I0654407

C. James Kelly

The Elephant Slayer

© 2015, C. James Kelly

Some Reading Required Co.

THE ELEPHANT SLAYER

At the time of this novel, it is predicted that if poaching of elephants continues at the rate it is today, they will be extinct in ten years.

TUSC

(Taskforce to Uncover Systems of Cabal)

THE ELEPHANT SLAYER

A giant orange sun had lit up the sky like a star gone nova as the rotation of the earth slowly pushed the darkness onto the savanna. The day had been long and the heat extreme as the herd ambled its way across the plain to the watering hole where they would spend the night. They had drank and bathed in the cooling water of the ponds, covering themselves with mud to keep the flies and gnats at bay and ate their fill of the lusher reeds and trees that surrounded the oasis. Now the elephants huddled just inside the tree line not ten yards from the water led there by the matriarch. Some dozed in the still heated air of the African evening, others grazed before sleep trying to ingest the last of the four hundred pounds of vegetation they would need to sustain themselves on the next day's trek. As they slowly began to drift off, some kept a trunk or an ear over a loved one while the smaller newborns instinctively leaned against their mothers while they dreamt of green pastures and succulent bamboo.

The matriarch stood watch but she felt at ease. There had been no signs of humans at the watering hole and she could detect no human stink in the breeze as it wafted through the trees on its way to the other side of the world. Eventually, her eyes closed as the last purple-orange rays slipped away and the dark humid night closed in around them like a damp blanket. She had been around a long time, sixty years to be exact. She had seen the encroachment of man with his ever-expanding fields of corn and cane. She had seen drought and flood. She had seen the birth of as many as two hundred calves. Still, she guided the herd from watering place to watering place, the trail memorized over the years, her huge tusks so long they almost touched in the middle as they curved out from her maw, always led her true. She was big for a cow, topping the scales at just over seven thousand pounds. There wasn't much that frightened her and she had always protected her herd even at her own peril. She could not know that this would be her last sunset.

~

The men had lain downwind of the ponds since the early morning. Even though they had tracked this herd for a couple of months, they weren't exactly sure of when the elephants would arrive. This was the perfect spot. Miles from the nearest village, so far gone that no one would hear the rifle reports. They had smeared themselves with the droppings of a previous herd of elephants that had used the tranquil hideaway to feed and water the day before so none of the seven smelled any too sweet after baking in the hot sun all day.

Their position was about one thousand Yards from the water's edge. The distance was pushing the accuracy range of their two Barrett M107 sniper rifles but they had found this method of hunting very effective in the past. The guns were the best money could buy and there position was slightly uphill with tall savanna grasses hiding them from anything or anyone looking up the hill. They had been here before and they felt confident in their position. As the day dragged on, they took turns searching the vast grassland with field glasses watching for any movement that would the signal the arrival of the herd. Finally, around midday a lumbering hulk appeared out of the tall grass and trees close to the horizon, shortly followed by the females and calves that made up the fifteen member family of elephants they had been waiting for.

TUSC

TUSC was not part of any government organization like the CIA or the Secret Service. If investigated, it would never be found to have been some huge underground group of crazed shirts trying to rid the world of the great evils that lurked in every nook and cranny just waiting to destroy the USA. TUSC had no floors of offices, no overseers, no chain of command and no authorized plan of action. There were no documents that could lead anyone to a source, no secured or bunkered fail-safe rooms or tech centers full of computers and agents and no paper trail that one could follow to an end. Although the operation had an overseer, no one knew who he was, in fact, TUSC was really just one man.

~

On October 23, 1983, two truck bombs struck separate buildings in Beirut, Lebanon. Dubbed the Beirut Barracks Bombings, the two blasts killed 241 U.S. and 58 French peacekeepers. From that time, the U.S. government relentlessly pursued any and every terrorist threat against America. Though many of the retaliatory sorties against known threats and actual acts of terrorism were televised over twenty years of chasing the jihadists, the Muslim extremists, the suicide bombers and the just plain crazies, nothing was ever leaked to the press of one of the most effective programs in combating terrorism in the free world. The tracking down and dismantling of terrorist financial networks and the pursuit of those who ran the front companies that willingly supplied terrorists with funds. For that, the United States created a special agency called the Office of Terrorism and Financial Intelligence.

At first, the money trails were fairly predictable. Find the drugs and the distributors dig out their banks and money launderers and you could effectively shut down the source of the terrorist's income. As time and technology went on terrorist networks made themselves aware of government efforts to stall their illegal activities and methods for funding terrorist acts met and exceeded the government's efforts to find them out and turn them off.

September 11, 2009, changed the policy again as the government of the United States began actively and openly shutting down and freezing assets they deemed to be used for and or part of a terrorist act or organization. Though efforts increased terrorist funding and accumulation of wealth seemed a never-ending battle. For every million seized ten were generated. Where was the money coming from?

MADDISON WISCONSON

Matthew Buxton had grown up in Maddison Wisconsin. The winters sucked and the summers were hot and dusty. His parents weren't educated. Dad worked part-time at the Dane County Farmers Market and mom pushed a broom at the University of Wisconsin Hospital.

He was a scrawny kid so he got shoved around a lot in public school. Luckily he had a good pitching arm so that stopped when he got to high school and began pitching for the Madison Mallards Baseball club. His days in Maddison were numbered though. Mat couldn't wait to get the hell out of Dodge. He knew there was more to life than pitching ball for a third-rate baseball team and helping his dad clean up after the weekend rush at the market. No, Mat had bigger plans and they would all start the second he got to Chicago which would be about two seconds after his last class at West High.

~

His first day in Chicago, Matthew woke up in a puddle surrounded by the trash and the refuse of the city theatre district. His balls felt like they had been kicked up into his forehead and he was drenched through to his underwear. The worst part was his backpack with all his clothes and his wallet was gone. The wallet which held everything he had saved to get set up in the big city had been stolen. He hadn't even had time to react. Two guys just pushed him into a side alley as he walked along the street and that was it. One had hit him behind the ear with something heavy and it was lights out.

The worst part was the embarrassment. He hadn't been there more than six hours. Just a quick walk through the theatre district was all he was going to do before finding a hotel. Now he was an inch deep in an alley puddle with no coat and no money. One thing for sure, he was not going back. It was only one hundred and fifty miles home to Maddison but there was no way he was going to give up. He had scoffed at his mother and fathers insistence that the big city would eat him up. What the hell did they know? They had lived in Madison for twenty-five years and had never been past the LEAVING MADDISON sign out on highway 90. One other thing, he had made his mind up about that day in the alley. He was never going to get fucked over again. The next time some thug was looking for an easy mark, it would be a most unfortunate day for them.

Matt picked himself up. He was damp and angry but he had never been one to wallow in self-pity. As he stepped out of the alley, the Chicago day was going by as usual for most people. Businessmen and women hurrying here and there, scurrying down the subway entrances like little moles trying to escape the sun. City buses lined up at the curb left the pungent stench of diesel behind as each, in turn, snatched their passengers from the curb and headed off to who knows where. Even the doughy aroma of pizza wafting down from one of Chicago's famous deep-dish pie stands did little to mitigate the aching in his balls and the chill beginning to fill the air as the day began to slip towered night.

Matt made his way to the pizza stand to ask the proprietor the directions to the nearest police station.

"Excuse me." Matt's voice showed no hint of what had happened to him. "Can you tell me where the nearest Police Station is?"

The vendor's quick look turned into an all-knowing stare. "Got mugged did ya?" he shot back.

"It's that obvious is it?"

"Yup, seen it a million times around here. Just new to the city son?"

"Sorry to say just a few hours. Can you get me to a police station so I can complain and maybe dry out?"

"I can do that and one better. The police are just

about two blocks that way. You can't miss it. It's got a big sign over the door that says Chicago Police Department and at this time of day about twenty white and blue cruisers out front. They probably won't do much for you though. They likely heard your story a few times today already. The other thing is if you go another two blocks on the same side of the street, there is a drop in center. It's full of bums and drunks and homeless but it's clean and you'll get a free meal and a shower. Not to mention a crappy cot to sleep on but better than out on the street overnight. That might cost you more than what you just lost. Best bet, go there first so you know you can get in. In another hour the place will be full. Hope that helps?"

Matt couldn't have asked for much more. He thanked the guy and made his way the four and a half blocks to the shelter picking his way through the crowds of people on their way home from work or just getting out for a bite before an early show.

MURDER

The three stars of Orion's belt were barely visible in the twinkling brilliance that was the African midnight sky. Night predators wandered in search of some unfortunate animal left partially consumed by one of the Savanna's larger carnivores. The cool breeze coming up from the plains to the watering hole kept the herd aerated and calm as they slept through the night.

The matriarch had been sleeping while standing on her feet for sixty years so when the bullet slammed into the side of her head just behind the left eye and just in front of her ear, she didn't fall over. It had penetrated her skull tearing into her brain and severing the nerves in her spinal column, essentially killing her instantly while paralyzing her at the same time.

Because of the silenced guns the poachers were using, there had been no loud report to spook the heard so the elephants slept on not realizing that their mother and overseer was gone.

Another round slammed into her side just behind the shoulder but with no result. She was already dead and still unmoved.

The poachers looked at each other in disbelief. This had never happened before. With their night vision binoculars, they could clearly see that the rounds had flown true. There should have been some result. The animal should be on the ground. There was no way any one of them was going to approach a herd of elephants in the middle of the night and wake them up to see if their bullets had hit their mark. Sunrise was only a few hours away they would just have to wait and see what the dawn would bring.

The heard slept on not realizing that their leader was gone.

~

The little one woke up as the sun breached the horizon bringing its warmth to the savanna for a new day. The winds throughout the night had blown the smell of blood from their deceased leader upwind as the herd slept on unaware of the death.

She was not old enough to understand the smell and it was only bad timing that as she pushed against the legs of her grandmother in her usual morning greeting the wind changed and the herd caught the stench of death.

The little ones good morning ritual shoving was

enough to topple the old elephant and as her body came crashing down. The rest of the herd understood what had happened and a warning trumpet from the trunk of one of the older members sent the panicked group stampeding, the smallest, confused and frightened, trying to keep up.

The poachers had been watching the heard since the first rays of daylight had brought the watering hole into view. When the herd bolted, they knew that they only had a small window of opportunity to retrieve their prize before the elephants returned to mourn their dead. An angry African elephant is something none of them wanted to encounter up close even if they had high powered rifles.

The group of men quickly broke down their camp and jumped into the all-terrain vehicles. Once at the water's edge, they wasted no time. Though the location was remote, there was always a chance that rangers could discover their illegal shoot and arrest or even kill them.

The machetes had been honed over last night's fire and were perfect for the gruesome work at hand. With very few chops, the giant tusks of the matriarch were wrenched from her face leaving it shattered and torn. Now the other predators would come. Not for the money, they could glean from the remnants of the carcass but for the sustenance that it would welcomely provide in the hostile environment they lived in.

The poachers had tossed the tusks into the back of their SUV's. It would be a long and dangerous journey from the grasslands and their hunting grounds to Bertoua, Cameroon the hub of the illegal ivory trade in Africa but the money they would make from their ill-gotten prize would feed their families for most of the year.

Their backs to the east the poachers did not see the returning herd of elephants as they huddled around their fallen leader and friend. Gently touching her now mutilated body and making low throat noises as they began to mourn the passing of their once strong and beautiful matriarch. They would spend a few hours covering the body with leaves and sticks before leaving, following their ancient path behind the next oldest female in line just as they had for centuries.

CHICAGO BLUES

Matthew's first night in Chicago wasn't exactly as he had planned after being robbed and his jacket taken he had then been directed to the local hostel by a pizza stand attendant. He was cold, broke and thoroughly pissed off and his mood didn't lighten after gaining entrance to the hostel.

The place was an old office building built in the eighteen hundreds. In those days, each floor was just a wide open space with desks arranged in long rows. Here employees would prepare tax returns or whatever they had been assigned to do for eight or nine hours before dragging their sorry asses home just long enough to eat and sleep before coming back to perform the exact same exercise the next day. It was depressing. The bright lights intended to help with reading and to keep employees alert felt more like an integration technique by the end of an eight hour day. The entire building had been wrapped in windows on every floor but the lower two-thirds had been blocked with curtains or paint to keep the workers from daydreaming lending to the air of imprisonment that the worn wood floors and the bare steel girders that were the backbone of the place oozed. There wasn't anyone around from that era to give an accounting of the lives spent hunching over those desks or hanging from a knotted rope when the soul-crushing heartache of the place took its toll. If asked, even back then employees would tell you there were ghosts in the place.

It had been renovated in the nineteen twenties into a ten-storey apartment building but as the city grew away from the downtown core the building fell into disrepair and was eventually abandoned. Windows were broken out and left to the elements, it soon became a haven for the lost, the homeless and the drug dealers of the time. A city initiative in nineteen seventy-five to try and help the growing homeless population brought a team of engineers and planners to the property to bring it back to life as a hostel for those without a roof over their heads.

That was the seventies and it was likely a pretty progressive place back in those days but this was nineteen ninety-five and the building had seen better days. Maybe the funding had fallen short in the last few years or maybe the people in charge just didn't give a shit but it was looking pretty run down.

Matthew had seen the homeless before but only on TV. He was surprised at how many worn out, bedraggled and seemingly disinterested men and women there were about. Some just standing in groups smoking, others sitting on the sidewalk backs against the wall while still others panhandled anyone who happened buy that looked like they might have a dime or two to spare.

He wasn't sure what was worse, the smell or the feeling of hopelessness that came over him when he saw the condition of his fellow inmates.

He had signed in at a front desk much like a hotel except with bulletproof glass. He was given a meal ticket and told to ask the door person on level two for a place to sleep. He had some hope at that point but it was quickly dashed when he got off the elevator and saw the squalor, not of the surroundings, they weren't ideal but of the inhabitants of the streets that called this place home every night they could get in.

The doorman pointed to a cot against the wall about halfway up the room. There were three sections of cots separated by aisles. Each cot had its own folding chair that doubled as a clothes rack and a place to sit what belongings one might have. At the far end there appeared to be a soup line. That was a guess as it looked conspicuously like the buffet at the Legion back home. If Matt's dad had a particularly good day at the market he would spring for dinner for the two of them there.

It might not have been perfect but whatever was simmering away at the hot plates did give off a not unpleasant aroma and Matthew, despite the trauma of the day, felt pretty damn hungry.

Not wasting any time he made his way to the line and pulled a plate, utensils and a tray together before adding himself to the row of shuffling bodies.

The food was good. He wondered if the place served breakfast too. These were fleeting thoughts for as soon as he finished his meal of chicken, carrots and mashed potatoes he fell asleep barely getting the plate and cutlery balanced on his chair before his head hit the tattered pillow. The last thought that ran through his head as the light faded away was, at least no one can steal my stuff while I sleep.

He slept like the dead and when he awoke, most of the hostel's patrons were away and gone. His body ached like he had gone ten rounds with Hulk Hogan. The lump on the back of his head was still pretty big and he had a massive headache. Not to mention the bruising he discovered while washing up in the community showers. Whoever had robbed him must have given him a few good boots while he was out. What kind of asshole would do that?

Mat cornered the attendee on duty, a new one from the night before. This one looked as uninterested as last night's dozy guardian.

"Hey, listen, do you have like a doctor on staff or someone who could take a look at my head. I got mugged yesterday and could really use a little help." He didn't expect to get much of a reaction but to his surprise, the guard gave him precise instructions on where the clinic was located in the building and where to fill out a report on the robbery.

The last part surprised him. Apparently, someone was running a task force to try and keep the homeless from being robbed of the little they had left.

He thanked the guard and headed down to street level where the clinic not only gave service to the inhabitants of the shelter but was also the medical access point for those in the community who couldn't afford health care to get advice and assistance.

There was a nurse and a couple of pages of forms to fill out before he could get someone to have a look at the bump on his head. Once he had filled in the blanks he handed the information back to the attendant behind the counter. He had turned to go back to his seat when she said. "One second there Matt is it?"

Mat turned, wondering what he could have filled out incorrectly.

"You put down a health care number here." It was more of a statement than a question.

"Yes." He answered. One thing his parents had always kept up was their family health care plan. He was damn grateful for it right now.

"We don't get a lot of people here with healthcare. You could go to one of the big clinics with this and get better care and service."

Matt spoke quietly as he told the nurse of his adventure from the day before. He just wanted to get someone to look at his head and maybe get a couple of aspirin before he went down to the police station to report it.

The nurse was sympathetic and said she would get him in as soon as she could, possibly about twenty minutes.

With time on his hands, Matt wandered the halls. The main floor of the hostel was dedicated to some community functions. In one room a woman was teaching a class of children about the Great Lakes, in another some elderly folks were being guided through the agony of building popsicle stick somethings, another a group was taking instruction from a man in a what looked like to Matt as a white bathrobe and pants held together with a black belt tied in a knot at the waist.

He was so intrigued with the sharp precise movements and rhythm of the class that he almost forgot his appointment at the clinic. He would get checked out, come back for more of whatever was going on.

~

What was going on was the morning martial arts class. Taught by Ethan Miller the class had been held on the premises of the hostel since nineteen eighty-one. Ethan had been a younger man then but had studied several forms of martial arts and was well on his way to becoming the Master that he was today.

Back then on an early morning in May, Ethan had been driving to work. His daily route took him north down Michigan Ave. all the way to Lake Shore Dr. where he had worked as a park attendant at the Oak Street Beach for the past three years. There was always a slowing down of the job through the winter but they still had lots to keep them occupied. Maintaining the rescue equipment, repainting the warning and information signs that were part of the everyday landscape of the beach and Ethan's favourite job of all repairing and painting the rescue boats that were strategically placed along the sandy shore of the beach just in case there was a need to go further out in the lake than swimming would allow.

Just the feel of the wood and using the woodworking tools that were required to update and maintain the wooden boats had a therapeutic effect on him. His biggest hope was that the boats would really take a beating so he would have more work to do on them throughout the winter months.

This particular day as he sipped his coffee and aimlessly stared out the window at the passing city landscape he witnessed three men kicking and beating someone outside of what looked like a large office building. His mother's words of warning were never "always wear clean underwear" they were always "don't get involved".

That, however, had never been Ethan's way. He could never turn a blind eye or a deft ear to the wrongs of the world and whether his presence brought a solution to every situation or not he was always the one to step in to try and set things right. His martial arts training gave him the confidence to do so more often than not. Today was no different.

He quickly pulled his car into the curb at the next open space and leapt from the door almost before it stopped. His sneakers, that were the standard issue of the beach community, a flat-topped deck shoe, made little sound as he ran towards the disturbance taking place in the middle of the sidewalk up ahead.

As he neared the four men, he assumed the one being pummeled was a man, he yelled, "Hey" a sharp expulsion of air forced the word to travel. It was not a nice hey like if you were greeting a friend, it was a demanding note that said WHAT THE FUCK IS GOING ON.

The three heads turned in unison. There was a look of surprise from all three that someone had accosted them but none of them chose to leave the chore at hand and run. Safety in numbers was likely the common thought.

Ethan was close enough now to see that the person on the ground was indeed a man but he couldn't tell if it was the beating that he was taking or if he was just down on his luck as his apparel looked more ragged than disheveled. Whatever the situation he could see that he was bleeding and not moving.

"Fuck off right now." The one nearest Ethan spoke first. "Unless you think you would like a bit of what this piece of shit is getting?"

"Yea hit the fucking road or we'll give you a bit of this too." The second guy didn't really have the conviction in his voice that the first one had, but together all three looked like pretty formidable opponents.

"Three against one isn't really fair is it?" Ethan

questioned. "Besides it looks like you can't do much more to him anyway."

"Well listen up then fucknuts." The first guy said, "We'll decide when we're done and you can get your nuts kicked into your throat if you want to wait around and keep poking your nose into other people's business."

"Ok then, well you better hurry up and get started because if you sit around here telling me what you're going to do much longer I am going to be late for work." Ethan countered.

Two of the men looked at each other in surprise. They probably hadn't had many people stand up to them and like most bullies in a pack, if someone did push back, they would readily fold up their tents and take a hike.

The one who acted like the leader was having none of it. Ethan's confidence had not swayed his intent. "Alright," he laughed, "let's see how tough you are. Common boys."

His two pals hesitated just long enough for Ethan to punch the charging lout so hard in the throat that he immediately dropped to the ground wheezing like an ancient vacuum cleaner that had never had the dust removed from its filter. He probably would have screamed if his vocal cords weren't crushed.

The ring leader's big mistake was assuming that Ethan was afraid of him. That led him to believe that he could just rush in and get the upper hand. His lumbering charge never took into consideration that Ethan expected him to do exactly what he was doing. With his attacker's defenses down, Ethan just ducked under the oncoming outstretched arms while at the same time driving the knuckles of his forefingers into the man's throat just under the chin. The power in the strike came from Ethan's legs as they pushed up from his crouched position and could have killed the would-be assailant if Ethan hadn't pulled the punch. As it was, this would be the last time the ringleader would try this stunt, at least with the ability to call for his friends to help.

The other two would be attackers were already putting time and space between their fallen buddy and themselves as they raced away down the street.

Ethan never looked twice at the fallen thug. He immediately rushed to the side of the man who had not moved from his place on the sidewalk.

As he turned the person over Ethan could see that he was most likely homeless. His clothing was in ill repair and his footwear showed signs of more than one occupant. Most disturbing of all was the obviously broken nose and the eyes that were already beginning to swell shut. Who knew how many other injuries he had sustained before Ethan had come to the rescue.

From his training at the beach, Ethan knew that moving him might harm him even further so he took a chance and left the man on the ground and entered the building directly beside the incident. Two heavy doors lead into a large reception area and he could immediately see that this was a place for the homeless. What it was or who the people were that occupied the halls were not what he was concerned with. There was a small reception desk off to one side of the entry and he made for that. Hoping that the person behind the desk could help.

"There's a man hurt right outside." He told the attendant.

The young woman who sat behind the desk looked like many of the younger people that the city hired to work the beaches in the summer. The city park programs offered a continuing educational employment program to those wanting to pick up extra credits for high school or college. There was a great demand for the jobs at the many beaches maintained by the city of Chicago and those primo jobs were usually picked up by the sons and daughters of those in the city with some social connection. Not to say that they didn't do the job once they were there but it often took prodding and a fair bit of coaching to get them to take the job seriously.

This was not one of those people. Without a word, her first reaction was to get on the phone to the police and asked for an ambulance. The operator must have asked her for the person's condition because she looked up at Ethan and relayed the question.

Ethan told her that "the man looked pretty beat up and that there was another that might need medical assistance and the police as well."

The information was passed to the operator and once finished with the call the young woman reached under the counter and pulled out a small medical kit. She then made a beeline for the front door with Ethan in tow.

The scene outside the building was much as Ethan had left it except maybe a couple of onlookers who weren't getting to close. It was better if you didn't see too much in this part of the city. All it would take much to become a person of interest to the police or a target of some gang if someone was to point you out as having been seen there.

Ethan quickly guided the woman to the victim of

the beating and she took great care in examining him where he lay. It would appear that she had some medical training. Her first reaction was to check for a pulse. Finding that, she then made a visual appraisal of the person before asking Ethan what had happened. Ethan told her how he had been driving by and had witnessed the person being beaten. He downplayed his part in the intervention but did include his part in taking out the ringleader at which the woman moved from the victim to the thug who was still on the ground unable to get enough breath to get up or speak.

"I know this person," she said. "He is not a good person nor is he the kind of person you want to get on the wrong side of. There are gangs in this neighborhood that like to prey on some of these homeless people. They do it just for fun because mostly no one fights back and they think it's funny to rob them of what little they have in this world. I mean they barely get from day to day why not take their dignity too? You had better go before the police and the ambulance gets here. I can handle this. It's not the first time this has happened. Please come back in a few days I would like to talk to you."

Ethan could actually see the wisdom in her words. He wanted to help but he also didn't want to become a target for some gang. He quickly thanked the girl and ran back to his car. The rest of his morning drive to work he reflected on the incident and tried to calm down after his encounter with the three muggers.

~

The week flew by. Ethan had driven home past the shelter where the mugging had taken place every day. He couldn't get the good-looking woman who had come to help the downed homeless man out of his head. He wasn't sure what was an appropriate amount of time before going back to see her but by Friday he was too curious to leave it until the following week.

After work, Ethan found a parking place about a block from the building just in case anyone had recognized his car from four days before. He felt confident that the only two witnesses to the event, the other two attackers, would keep their mouths shut about what happened. They wouldn't want anyone to know that they had been involved in the beating nor would they want to admit to their friends that one guy ran them off. He was also pretty sure it would be a long while before the ringleader would be talking at all.

Ethan didn't even know what the woman's name was and when he entered the foyer he could see that she was not behind the desk where he had enlisted her help days before.

The young man on duty this late Friday afternoon was as professional and well dressed as the young lady had been. "Can I help you?" he said as Ethan approached the desk.

"I am looking for someone who works here." He replied. "She was at this desk on Monday, blonde, maybe five seven, well dressed?"

"Yup, that's Kristy." He replied.

"Is she working today?" Ethan wasn't hopeful.

"Yup." He replied again. "Fridays is her day for helping in the kitchen, we rotate jobs to keep from going nuts. You can find her on the second floor. That's where the kitchen and some of the sleeping areas are."

Ethan thanked him and headed for the elevator down the hall from the front desk. His brief trespass into the building told a big story. He could see that the place was more than a hole for those less fortunate to hide in. There were children's hand paintings on the walls and the floors and walls looked to be clean and well kept. As he made his way down the corridor he could see that there were doors marked with numbers and given titles to announce what was within. Things like Day Care and Learn to Read. There was more going on here than just a place for the homeless and less fortunate to lay their heads for a night and get a free meal.

He found the elevator and headed up to the second floor. Even the elevator while old was clean and graffiti free. If someone was going do a little spray painting in a place like this it usually took place in the elevator out of sight of prying eyes.

To Ethan's surprise, he was met on the second floor by another well-dressed person this time in uniform. Not like a security guard or anything like that but you could see that the flannel gray pants and the starched white shirt along with a thick leather belt that held a flashlight, a small leather pouch and a keychain with a number of multi-colored keys gave off a feeling of authority. The patch on the breast pocket had a red and gold emblem that read Chicago Shelters and the person's name embroidered underneath.

As Ethan approached the attendant smiled and asked if they could do something for him.

Ethan imagined that he didn't look a lot like the usual customer for the second floor so he politely smiled back and inquired after Kristy.

"The person at the desk downstairs said I might find Kristy up here. I met her on Monday and she invited me to return for a chat."

"Ok." the person responded. "At the far end of the buffet line, you can see there is a door? That's the kitchen, just go in there and ask for her. It's a pretty big place but there are only about four chefs and the rest are volunteers. She shouldn't be too hard to find."

Ethan thanked the attendee and made his way to the back of the large room its walls conspicuous in their absence of décor. A dingy off-white, probably from years of over-painting, they held no fineries to make the place look anything more than a gym at best. Rows of beds lined the walls halfway down the room and then a number of rows of tables and folding chairs designating the dining room split the space in half.

Ethan followed the directions given to the door at the far end of the room. He opened it to a wonderful smell. The warm homey essence of bread baking in the oven and the aromatic, mouthwatering scent of garlic and basil that could only mean pasta sauce stewing on the stove. The kitchen was bright and full of energy. Chefs in white with the traditional toque blanche hat, heads down, intent on their recipes, the volunteers in jeans and tees covered by large white aprons, stirring big pots full of vegetables and cutting mountains of rolls in half.

Ethan spotted Kristy at the far end of the production line that was precisely organizing little squares of green and red Jell-O into tiny white paper muffin containers. As he walked over to her, he could see that the hygiene of the kitchen far outstripped the rest of the building. "Place is pretty spic and span." He announced. Her immediate reaction was a look of confusion but it was momentary as he could see the recognition come quickly to her face.

"Oh, it's you." She exclaimed. "I was wondering if you would show back up."

"Well, one doesn't turn down an opportunity to revisit such an endearing establishment."

"Well since you are being so smug we are just about to start today's dinner service so you can get on one of those aprons of the wall over there and start pitching in. We can use an extra pair of hands today."

The slightly upturned smile gave away her sense of humor hidden by the curt retort so Ethan played right along.

Clad in his new work uniform he returned to the Jell-O line and requested his first assignment. "I'm

Ethan." He said, holding out his hand. His greeting was met with rubber-clad hands held up in the universal sign for, can't right now I'm handling food. The two other volunteers at the counter chuckled under their breath.

"I'm just about done here and then we start loading up the service area. You can help by pulling out those large silver serving trays and then fill them up with the vegetables you see in those big vats of boiling water. There are carrots, green and yellow beans, and mashed potatoes. Start by filling each of those and then we can refill from there."

Ethan was only too happy to have busy hands. He made short work of the vegetable transfer and he was just finishing up when a loud bell rang three times. There was a glass window that opened out to the service area from the kitchen and he could see people starting to file in from the far end of the room. He turned from his post to find Kristy standing directly behind him.

"That is the call for the third floor to come for dinner." She said. "We run each floor individually so the occupants of each floor can return to their floor leaving the last group to get fed and then remain here where they will spend the night. You can push those trays out front and then keep filling them up until we run out of food."

"Do you run out a lot?" Ethan asked.

"Every day."

Ethan pushed his cart full of vegetables out to the serving line. As the people began to file in, he was overwhelmed not only by the wretchedness of some but by the overall order that pervaded the space with their arrival.

He spent the next hour and a half refilling and then serving on the line when that job ended. If he thought that would be the end of his labors he was mistaken. After helping to bring the large metal pans and serving trays back to the kitchen, he was promptly put to work washing and cleaning these and all the utensils involved in the evenings' service.

That job finally done, Ethan looked at his watch. It was well after eight o'clock and the sun would be down. That meant in this part of town he would have to be a little more alert heading back to his car.

"Well Ethan, I see you survived your first tour of duty at a shelter." A soft voice at his elbow woke him from his musings.

"Well it was an experience, I can tell you that, but I work with the general public on a daily basis and in some ways, this group is quite a bit more behaved."

That got a chuckle from Kristy. "Well tell you what, we have a little cafeteria downstairs that doesn't close until nine. Let me buy you a coffee and we can have a chat about the other day."

"Sounds good," Ethan replied and followed her to the elevator and down to the first floor.

"The place is relatively clean for a shelter." Ethan mused.

"That's because not only do we have strict city codes but we are trying to set a precedence. We offer other community services here other than feeding and sheltering the homeless. We want our facility to be and look professional as much as possible on the budget we are given by the city and the state."

"Yes, I saw some of the signs on the doors as I passed on my way up to the second floor. What other services to you offer here?" Ethan queried.

"Some are static like daycare and learning to read classes and others come and go depending on who can volunteer. We have a full-time medical clinic with a doctor and a nurse and we hold family planning, prenatal and domestic challenges classes every week. The café is the brainstorm of one of our wealthier contributors and I sometimes think the money could be better used elsewhere but on nights like this a hot coffee really helps keep you going so I'm not going to complain and it does generate some income and a paid position for one of our needing customers."

"Well, there is a lot more going on here than you would realize if you were just passing by on the street," Ethan said as they sat at a small round table. The café wasn't much, just four little round tables and chairs and a counter space with a few things like muffins and banana bread and a couple of pots brewing on a hotplate.

"Speaking of a lot going on." Kristy began. "How did you end up getting involved in Monday's trouble out front?"

"Fist tell me, how is the person that was mugged?" Ethan countered.

"Broken nose, a couple of swollen eyes and some pretty good bruising but he's ok, thanks to you. You served him tonight as a matter of fact."

That brought a look of surprise to Ethan's face. "You didn't say anything."

"Because it is a small community. It's amazing how fast information can travel and I didn't want to put you in a situation for retaliation."

"I appreciate that," Ethan said. "And I am glad the

person is ok."

"So tell me about Monday," Kristy asked again.

"Well, I was driving by on my way to work when I noticed three guys pummeling someone. Couldn't let that happen so I just parked and jumped in."

"So how did the bad guy get his throat punched in? The police say that he may not regain his voice."

"Well, that is unfortunate" Ethan's voice gave no hint of remorse. "I did ask them politely to stop what they were doing and I did give them fair warning. The man rushed me and I had no choice to defend myself. Since I didn't know if he intended to kill me or not I used as much force as I felt necessary to permanently subdue him."

"So are you ex-military or a Seal or something?"

"No, but I have studied martial arts most of my life and teach karate, Kung Fu and Aikido at some levels. It is unfortunate that that guy will have a hard time communicating for a while but the alternative would have meant my own injury."

"Well, I am not sure whether you are brave or stupid but thank you for looking out for one of ours," Kristy said.

"Not a problem. You know since you have space here in this building how about if I come by a couple of times a week and teach a few lessons. It sounds like these folks could benefit from some self-defense training. The exercise itself couldn't do them any harm either."

"That is a great idea and one that is sorely needed in this community but we have no budget left this year to take on any more activities." Kristy's voice hinted at her disappointment. She thought Ethan's kind gesture was the perfect type of program for the rough and tumble life led by the street people of this part of Chicago. Her assumption that his offer was motivated by money couldn't have been more wrong.

"I don't want any money," Ethan replied. "I have a job and would be happy to give beginning lessons to anyone who was interested. Why don't you ask around and see if the program would work and I can stop by again next week to see if we can do it?

"Wow, someone who doesn't care about money," Kim said.

"Oh, I care about money." Ethan jumped in. "Just not in this situation. Besides, it will give me an excuse to come see you again." He didn't know why he said that. Actually, he did. He really liked her. In the brief time, he had been at the shelter, he had seen how she interacted with her co-workers and the people they helped. She was beautiful there was no denying that and there was just something else about her demeanor that pulled him to her. He hoped he hadn't spoken out of turn.

"Well Mister Ethan, until next week then. Maybe you'll tell me your last name then too." There was a humorous twinkle in her eye that Ethan like.

"Maybe you'll tell me yours then as well." He quipped as they both stood up to leave.

Ethan walked out the front door and into the cool of the late evening air. His head was full of the experience at the shelter but he also kept a close watch as he made his way to his car. Once on the road, he reflected on the conversation he had had over coffee. He was looking forward to teaching at the center and to more time with Kristy.

MAN TRACKING

Matthew had gotten wind of the poachers from an old friend who worked at a group called the International Ranger Federation. The Rangers were the front line on poaching and often came under fire from poachers while doing their job. They were also witness to the atrocities leveled on the animals they had sworn to protect.

Matthew knew a number of the Rangers personally and relied on their Intel and information to find those who poached and subsequently those who profited from the sale of illegal animal parts. More specifically he used the information they passed along to follow a trail that would lead him to the terrorist organizations that were the beneficiaries of the sale of illegal elephant ivory.

This time he had flown into Berthoud, Cameroon, days ahead of the poachers who had murdered the ancient matriarch of the elephant herd. After renting a car he drove to within a kilometer of the outskirts of the nearly one hundred thousand occupant city. Here, where reasonably well-kept homes started to become intermingled with the tents and shanties that housed the poorer residents, he pulled down a side street and parked the vehicle under a tin roof held up by four slender and somewhat fragile looking hardwood posts. After covering the car with a tarp that lay beside the makeshift carport, he unlocked a door in the wall of the building adjacent to his vehicle. Painted the exact same color as the one-story adobe dwelling it was inconspicuous and opened into a one bedroom, kitchen and living room with a bathroom. The bathroom had a shower, a luxury that was only possible because of the water tank on the roof that captured rain which could be as much as two hundred millimeters in a month. Something that the local population would usually watch, soak into the desert sand before ever thinking that they could use it for drinking or any other purpose.

He had been here before, many times. This was his staging area and he took great pains to keep it under the radar and well stocked. It blended in with all the other small dwellings in the neighborhood and he rarely ventured outside its walls in the daytime.

Today was an exception. He wanted to get eyes on the poachers as soon as they entered the city. There was only one road from where they had killed the elephant to Bertoua and he wanted to be there when they showed up. From that side of the city the road rose up to the north and he would be able to see them coming for miles giving him enough head start to retrieve his rental and follow them to where they would rendezvous with those who would pay them for their ill-gotten prizes. Hey knew that they would move the ivory, after cutting it into more manageable pieces, to the port city of Douala. From there the ivory would be sold and then the tusks themselves would be smuggled out of the country concealed in any manner of ways in one of the hulking cargo ships that left the port every day. The money secreted away to an agent of one terrorist group or another. This was where Matthew's job had no rule. Situations would determine how he moved forward from that point. He relied on instinct and his many years of training starting with his indoctrination into the martial arts on a fateful trip to Chicago in the early seventies to joining the American Armed Forces and become a Navy Seal. He had managed forty-six ops on the continent and he was field tested and ready. He spoke the local dialect like a native and could work his way around a bunch more. He had stopped a shit load of money getting into the hands of the wrong people and he was going to keep doing it until both ends of the equation dried up. Once the terrorist no longer had access to the funds from the ivory sales there would be less of a market for those willing to take the risk of killing, mutilating and transporting the ivory from elephant tusks. With over one hundred thousand elephants killed in less than three years, if someone didn't do something they would be gone soon anyway. Matthew was determined to not let that happen and even more determined to stop the loonies who benefited from the sale of ivory that aided their extremist intent.

Once inside the dwelling, Matthew changed from his European styled traveling clothes to more local attire. A tee shirt and canvas shorts with a pair of sandals were topped off with a well-worn ball cap with the words CO-OP on the front. You couldn't tell him from a local unless you got close enough to see that he didn't have the hardened calluses on his hands of a worker nor the pan-fried body color that the African sun eventually imposed on anyone living in that part of the world for very long.

Bertoua was a melting pot. Every color and creed. Locals mostly wore a casual European style of dress. On hot days, the merchants and the general population were to a man dressed in shorts and tees while the woman wore skirts. The businessmen downtown typically wore suits, mostly grey or black with a white shirt and more often than not brown shoes.

The tribal influences were more prominent on the outskirts where the tents and shanty tin-roofed dwellings were home to the laborers and the people who worked at menial jobs in town cleaning or with the city work department. Others had jobs in the market. Every day a beautiful line of colored African wraps mixed with the kaki brown of the workers shorts and sandals made its way from the outskirts to their respective points of labor or the closest bus stop and back again as the heat of the afternoon sun began to ease and the day wore down returning to their waiting families.

The cacophony of skin types and colors made it easy for Matthew to blend in. No one would suspect he was anything other than just another one of the hundreds who passed along the dusty road that led out of town on their way to who knows were.

That's how it went. Once he had changed he merely walked to the end of the street, turned left and followed those on their methodical journey to and fro.

In twenty minutes he had found a large hardwood tree on the edge of town. Its overhanging limbs were perfect to keep the sun from baking his skin and he had a clear view of the road coming down from Boulembe and the Central African Republic. With his back resting against the giant trunk he periodically watched the road through a small set of field glasses keeping the lenses under the brim of the ball hat he wore so no reflecting light would give the long traveling poachers a heads up that someone might be watching them.

They were easy to spot. Traffic along the dirt

highway was typically on foot and what was motorized was mostly farm vehicles. One ton trucks with makeshift wooden sides covered with a tarp to keep whatever produce was being hauled to the markets in town from the blazing heat of the sun. The rest were late model sedans, usually in ill repair and taking their time to avoid the many potholes of the poorly maintained route and to conserve gas, which was a luxury and only used with purpose not for kicking around on a Friday night like back in the states.

The open-sided SUV that Matthew was watching was still a few kilometers away but through his field glasses he could tell that they weren't too worried about how much gas they used as the speed with which they were traveling was kicking up a pretty good cloud of dust in their wake and every so often they would hit a pothole that would send the two sitting on the tailgate airborne. If it wasn't for the surrounding roll cage they would have lost a couple of their crew before they got to town.

Most telling of all was the tarp that covered something big in the back. So big in fact that it extended out between the two anchormen on the gate where the material whirled and flapped violently in the wind generated by the speed.

Matt had seen this before. These guys were brazen. They barely cared that they were transporting an illegal substance and had probably done it so many times that they were overconfident. Confident enough that they thought they were untouchable. Confident that no one would stop them or try to rob them because they had been here before and they had guns.

Matthew was pretty confident that they would beg for mercy before he was done with them. He wasn't going to kill them or torture them for information. Either option was useless. One would accomplish nothing except take a couple of poachers out of the mix. They would quickly be replaced. The other would not reveal any information he did not already know. He only needed them to show him where they were taking the ivory for sale. That was the information he needed so he could follow the next link in the chain. What they would be begging him for was not to turn them into the police. Poaching was a crime punishable by imprisonment in this part of Africa. Sometimes as long as sixteen years. Most of the population looked upon the elephants as national treasures, even the criminals. Anyone who found themselves in prison for poaching elephant ivory would not be in prison for long. The death rate for that particular offense was about one hundred percent and not in a nice way. The imprisoned poacher was usually stomped to death within the first twenty-four hours of being jailed.

Matthew got back to his bungalow with about ten minutes to spare. He pulled an old motor scooter from behind the couch and dragged it out under the carport that now housed his rental car. It was an old Honda Hobbit 50, worn and dented, the leather of the seat was shredded where a thousand asses had slipped and sat over countless miles of dusty African trail. Matt had bought it from his neighbor when the man's father died and they needed extra money to leave the country for his funeral. It ran like a charm mostly because Matt had rebuilt the engine. Bringing in parts from a stopover in England he had spent a rainy weekend tearing it down and rebuilding it to make sure it was a reliable transport. He thought for his purpose it would be less conspicuous than the rental.

Matthew chatted with a passerby as he sat on his bike and watched the road behind him in the little round rear view mirror attached to the left handlebar. He saw the truck he was waiting for a few blocks back. He didn't have to panic. It had slowed to a crawl in amongst the general populous traveling on its way to the inner city. He watched as it passed from under the brim of his hat not even glancing in that direction until they had gone up and over a nearby hill in the road. Then he said goodbye to the

young woman he had given thirty francs to have a
conversation with for a few minutes and took off
after the four poachers.

THE BEGINNING

Matthew was let in to see the doctor a couple of minutes after his tour of the ground floor of the hostel. He was surprised to see how clean and well-kept it was. He could see that they had as much modern equipment as any up to date clinic and he actually felt quite at ease with his surroundings. The doctor was not some old geezer as he had half expected. He looked to be in his mid-thirties and well groomed. His bedside manner was much as Matt had been used to back home and after a thorough inspection of Matt's head wound, he let Matt know that it was a nasty bump but it didn't need stitches. It would probably be sore for a few more days and would likely heal a lot faster than Matt's ego. Matt agreed and took a small bottle of aspirin before thanking the doctor and finding his way out into the street. His first intent was on making a report of the robbery to the police even though he was quite certain that there would be no recourse. He didn't see who had mugged and robbed him and his meager belongings were not distinguished enough to be recognizable. They probably tossed everything in his backpack and just kept the money.

That was a thought though. He decided to take a

quick look around the alley and area where his adventure had started and see if there was anything left behind.

He passed the police station on the way and made a note to get back there as soon as he finished his search. The alley was a lot closer to the police than he had remembered from the day before. He entered the gloomy space between the two buildings with some trepidation but he was determined to see if his assailants had left him anything useful. He kept an eye in his rear view mirror so to speak, taking quick glances behind every few steps. The further he progressed the more aware he became of his surroundings. Trash bins piled with the night before refuse stank the place up with the rot of whatever was on the other side of the two walls he was surrounded by. There were larger dumpsters too. He pulled himself up on everyone until he came to a big blue bin about halfway down the alley. As he peered over the edge, he could see his backpack down in the mix of cardboard and trash. Jumping in, he found that his belongings were in tack. Apparently, all that his foes were interested in was the cash he had been carrying. That was something. At least he could wash his clothes and be able to change into something clean.

He quickly scrambled out of the bin and headed for the entrance. He hadn't realized how jumpy he was until he was back on the street. His hands were shaking and his mouth was dry.

It went just as he had suspected with the police. After filling out a litany of paperwork and answering a few questions from one of Chicago's least interested men in blue, he was out on the street and wondering what his next move should be. He wasn't hungry because the hostel had served breakfast. Then he remembered the strange class going on in the room back at the shelter. He had meant to go and check that out. Might as well start there. Maybe they also had some kind of counseling or even a job around the place. He wasn't afraid to work if he could make a little money.

~

The drop in center almost felt like home when he returned to the glass doors that welcomed strangers one and all to the shelter. Two days ago, you would have flabbergasted Matt if you had of told him that he would be relying on the generosity of others to survive. Basically homeless still, here he was.

He made his way down to the room where he had witnessed the workout session taking place that morning before he had gotten sidetracked with the alley and the police. It was now empty except for the man he had seen leading the group. He had discarded his strange outfit and was clad in a more normal blue jeans and a long sleeve cotton shirt. Except for the fact that he had no footwear and was barefoot, he looked like any other man on the street.

Matt poked his head around the door and said. "Hi." The man looked up and invited him in.

"Hi." He responded. "Please take your shoes off and come in."

"Matt took off his shoes, repositioned his newly recovered backpack and made his way over to the folding chair the man was sitting on."

He had been working on some paperwork which he transferred from his lap to the floor as Matt approached.

"Ethan Miller." The man held out his hand. He was tall, maybe six feet and Matt could tell by his grip that there was muscle to go along with the height.

"Matthew Buxton." Matt returned taking the proffered hand.

"I noticed you teaching some kind of class here this morning and it looked interesting. I come from a small farming community and I don't think I have ever seen anything like it."

"Well, it's a martial arts class that I give here at the shelter. We've been holding the classes for almost ten years now. If you're using the facilities here, you're welcome to come and take part."

"I am here temporarily I guess," Matt responded. "I got mugged yesterday, my first day in town and ended up being directed to this facility for the night. I'm still trying to find my way and figure out how I'm going to survive. The muggers took all my money but today I went back to the alley where it happened and managed to retrieve some of my belongings. I guess muggers have no use for clothes and personal effects."

"That happens a lot in this neck of the woods," Ethan explained. "That is one of the reasons we hold the classes. These guys prey on those weaker than themselves and they don't care if the person has something or nothing, they take whatever the person has of value and leave the rest. Most of the people in this place have very little but they take it anyway. Every once in a while they run into one of our more experienced trainees and they get a surprise. I just wish I could get more of them to see the value in the lessons. Not just for self-defense but the commitment to the training often gives them a new perspective going forward for jobs and life."

It sounded very interesting to Matt not just because he was determined to never get mugged again but he liked the idea of it being a starting point. Something he could learn for protection but also something that sounded like it might have some social value as well. Little did he know that meeting was going to shape his entire life.

"I think I will probably be here for a bit till I can sort myself out so if it's ok with you I'd like to give it a try," Matthew said.

"Always good to have a new recruit," Ethan responded. "Class starts at ten every morning. First rule. No shoes in the dojo. That's what we call this space when we are using it for training. If you like the art I will teach you anything you would like to know about it including weapons and hand to hand if you get that far. You won't need a Karategi to start, you can just wear a T-shirt and a pair of shorts if you have them. If you stick with it, we will make sure you get the proper clothing to participate. See you in the morning." Ethan held out his hand one more time and Matt shook it.

It was funny but after having talked to Ethan, he felt a sense of relief. He had a starting point. Maybe it wasn't the greatest start but the shelter had a bed and food and until he could find his way, he was safe. He would make sure that he would be there on time for his first lesson in the morning. Things were looking up as he headed back to the front desk to see what his options were for staying at the shelter for a few more nights.

~

The front desk referred him to one of the social workers supplied by the city. The social workers were mostly trainees coming from recent university and college courses for training. Twice a month a true city social worker would be in attendance to report on how the shelter was working with those interested in programs and to make sure they were meeting the city requirements in order to maintain their funding.

Matt had been led down a hall behind the reception desk and ushered into a small waiting room where two chairs and a coffee table containing some very used magazines were the only items of interest except for an adjoining door from which he could hear muffled conversation. Matt could only assume that the voices were those of the person he would be talking to and one other. So left to his own devices, he perused the collection of magazines splayed out on the table. The dates on the covers were six months old but that didn't matter. They were mostly Hollywood rags reporting on who was getting thin, who starred in what new movie and who was finally getting divorced after years of public fighting and sleeping around.

He had just finished a very interesting article on whether or not a certain Hollywood starlet had got breast implants when the door to the inner office opened and a ragtag gentleman followed by a young woman in a fairly nice pantsuit came through.

"Let me know if that contact works for you, Bill." The woman said.

"I will and thanks for the hand up." The man replied. The guy took a quick glance at Matt as he left and the woman invited Matt in.

She had a clipboard in her right hand and Matthew assumed that it was the information he had filled out the day before.

"Come in Mr. Buxton." She offered. Matt followed her into a sparsely furnished smallish office with a central desk piled with paperwork and coffee cups, a couple of folding chairs strategically placed in front of it and a very used couch pressed into the wall to the left. The right wall contained ancient filing cabinets that took up its entire length and lent a sense of bus stop to the place.

Matthew took a seat in one of the folding chairs and waited for the woman to scan through his information.

"Well Matthew, my name is Nora. Looks like you had a pretty rough day yesterday."

"Yes, mam," Matt replied. Even though Nora didn't look that old, he had always been taught to respect anyone who was offering a service, especially if they were offering for free."

"You can call me Nora. Mam makes me feel old." Nora had a little smile on her face which led Matt to believe he hadn't made a bad first impression.

"Unfortunately, you would be surprised at how many people we get in here that are new to town and new to the challenges a big city can provide. You are not the first victim of street violence that has passed along these halls."

"Yea, I talked to Ethan a few minutes ago and he informed me of much the same thing," Matt replied.

"So you talked to Ethan?

"Yes, I saw his class this morning on my way out to report my mugging to the police and to see if I could retrieve anything of my belongings from the alley."

"Ethan is a good guy. He provides a vital service to the people who frequent this place. This is a dangerous part of the city at night and anything we can do to help people defend themselves is a good

59

thing. So how are you feeling and what can I do for you?"

"I'm good," Matthew said. "My head has settled down and I still have a few aspirins left from your medic. I was just wondering what the timeline is for staying here. Do I have to register for so many days if I want to stay more than just day to day or do I have to just show up every afternoon to make sure I can get in?"

"It looks to me like you are not a typical homeless person. So if your intention is to use the center as a base till you can get on your feet then you can register for a month at a time and will always have a bed." Nora shuffled some papers on her desk and pulled a blue cardboard envelope out of the pile. We currently only have fifteen occupants who are using the monthly status so you should be good to go. Just register at the front desk with whoever is on duty today and I will authorize your request."

"Thanks," Matthew replied. "That really helps and takes the pressure and worry off."

"Not a problem. That's what we're here for."

Matthew stood up and headed for the door. Nora followed him to the front desk and spoke to the attendant on duty.

"Good luck. " Nora said as she headed back to her office leaving Matt hunched over the forms that would allow him to stay as a resident at the shelter.

~

The following day after Matthew had spent his first night as a resident, he hurried to be on time for his first morning of training with Ethan Miller. He was surprised by the turnout. He counted the bodies in the room and he thought fifteen was a pretty big number for a place that housed mostly people whose only interest was staying alive day to day.

Some of the attendees were robed in the white uniforms he had seen on the previous morning including Ethan. The garment consisted of a pair of baggy pants and a stylized top that was held closed with varied colored belts tied at the waist. Matt would find out later that the belts represented a person's level of achievement or grade.

He did feel a little self-conscious as he had never taken part in any sport that was individual. Most of his athletic endeavors had been team based like baseball and football, the standard American sports. This was his first adventure into a solo sport and he felt a little isolated.

He was surprised to feel a tap on his shoulder that

made him start. Whether he would admit it or not, he was still a little jumpy after his experience in the alley two days ago.

"Glad you could make it." Ethan had appeared as if by magic at his side.

"Oh, yea, I thought I would get right into it since I got them to let me stay for a month until I can sort my situation out." Matt stammered.

"That's great. Let me give you a few tips for your first time. We always start with some meditation and then a warm-up, then we review some basic moves. Some of the students have mastered these moves, so follow me and don't get distracted because others are not doing what I do.

Follow along as best as you can but don't try to keep up if you fall behind also don't try to do anything that feels too hard. Trust me, you will get it after a time if you stick with it.

The class is usually an hour but it sometimes goes longer especially if we have a couple of sparing matches after.

I teach each group individually to their level of expertise. You are the only new person today so you will be the lucky one with my personal attention."

Matt thought that it could be good and bad. He did

feel a lot calmer for the advice but he was anxious to see how he would fit in.

Matt saw Ethan move to the center of the room. Up until now, Matt was surprised by the lack of hubbub. The room was eerily quiet for a gym. One of the other students called. "Line up."

Matt, not knowing where to stand took up a place at the back. Ethan then stepped in front of the group and everyone bowed except Matt. Well, he did bow but only after he saw the rest do so.

Ethan clapped his hands and the group fanned out in even rows.

As the lesson progressed, Matt struggled through the warm-up. Back, neck and hip rotations with many other stretches designed to loosen up the body for exercise seemed endless and many left him panting.

He was determined to not let the difficulty deter him. Matt knew from his work with his father that something new could not be mastered at once but would become normal over time.

After the stretching, Ethan separated the fifteen students into groups. Matt now saw that they were organized by the color of their belts. He was left alone while each group was given a set of movements to complete. As the groups got into their respective rhythms, Ethan came to where Matt was standing. Ok Matt, this being your first day, there are just a few rules to go over and then I will give you your first lesson in Karate.

The most important rule of the dojo is behavior. Poor behavior will not be permitted. You must be respectful of everyone here and those that come after you.

Next, you must bow to the Shomen. This is the little shrine you see at the back of the room. It doesn't matter how many times you come and go from the dojo, you will always bow to the Shomen. You do this when you reach the entrance or door to the dojo. You face the Shomen, feet together, keep your legs straight, your arms should be at your sides and touching the sides of your thighs, your hands should be open and facing downward along the seam of your gi with your fingers and thumb together. To bow, bend forward at the waist to about 45 degrees, keep your eyes looking downward and do not let your arms move or leave your side, pause for a second at the bottom of the bow then unbend. The entire bow should take only a few seconds, but it should be performed with the utmost courtesy and respect.

Never arrive late.

At the beginning of each class, you will hear the lineup call. Always keep the senior students to your right.

These are a few basic rules and for now enough. I will write them down for you for your next class and I will bring a book. I have to help you understand some of the other many basic rules of the Dojo and Karate.

This is your first lesson so you need to understand balance. I will show you three variations on the stance and I want you to practice these today.

Ethan showed Matt three ways to stand. He called them The Walking Stance, The Front Stance, and the Cat Stance. He watched as Matt took up each individual stance and then moved on to the rest of the separated groups telling Matt to continue to rotate through each stance and try to find a position that felt comfortable in each.

As Ethan moved amongst the other students, Matt could hear him giving a correction or helping with placing a foot or arm in the correct position.

When the class was over, Matt had practiced the stance positions for over thirty minutes and while he felt like he had got the concept right off the bat, Ethan had not come back his way, so he continued to explore the subtleties of each position until the time was up. Again the same student called "Line up." Matt took his place at the back of the class. The class bowed and Matt followed suit. Some said thank you in English and some said something in what Matt assumed was Japanese. He figured it meant thank you as well.

The students filed out and as each left, they bowed to the Shomen. Matt did likewise. He had only taken a couple of steps outside the gym when he heard Ethan call his name.

"Matt, could you please return for a moment."

Mat thought maybe he had missed something on the way out but remembered to bow as he re-entered the dojo.

"Very interesting Matt," Ethan said. "It is pretty unusual for someone to walk out of the dojo after their first lesson and remember to bow on the way back in."

Mat had barely thought about it. His dad had been a pretty strict guy so you don't need to tell him one thing twice.

"It had not occurred to me, not to once you had

told me to." He replied.

"Again interesting that this is your thought. I wanted to commend you on your performance today. You seem to have an uncanny understanding of what we are doing here for someone who has never been exposed to Karate before."

"I understand respect," Matt replied.

"That may be so but almost every student I ever taught, including the great ones, never made it through thirty minutes of doing stances their first time without losing focus and looking around for something else to do."

"Well in my family if you lost focus or didn't finish your chores you could be sure you would hear about it. Let me tell you there is nothing harder to do than look in your mother's eyes when she's telling you why she is disappointed in you."

Ethan laughed. "Well, however you came by your work ethic it will do you well if you continue with Karate."

"I liked it. I liked the feel of the room and the students. I had a bit of a time with some of the warm-up moves but I think I will get it. I'll see you tomorrow."

"Great to have you with us, Matt," Ethan responded as he watched what he thought might be a new protégé walk to the door, turn and bow on his way out.

BERTOUA

The men in the four-wheel never looked behind them. It was as if they had done this so many times they didn't need to see if anyone was following or noticing their cargo. They had become complacent. Something Matthew would not be but it did make following the four men very easy.

He kept his distance. There weren't very many places they might turn off before they got to the city proper, so he lagged behind. Far enough to be inconspicuous but not so far that he couldn't see their vehicle or recognize the occupants. This wasn't his first rodeo but he didn't want to take any chances. His job was to find out who was paying for the ivory at this point and then follow them to their destination. He didn't know how many tradeoffs there would be or how long it would take him to discover those ultimately responsible for the trade or better yet the beneficiaries of the money made from the illegal sale of the tusks. That was his ultimate goal. To eradicate the organizations that survived by way of the money generated by poaching elephant ivory and to bring an end to not only the slaughter of innocent elephants but the slaughter and terrorizing of innocent men, women and children all over the world perpetrated by the terrorist organizations who used their ill-gotten funding to bomb, murder and subjugate all those who did not agree with their insane and radical ideologies.

Matt's little Honda meant that he had more maneuverability than the poachers so as they came within the city limits where the compacted dirt of the outer road turned to a potholed paved trail of the same well-traveled trail he moved a little closer to his prey, making sure they didn't get down a side street without him noticing. The men in the four by four still had not looked back and probably wouldn't until they did turn to their intended destination. When that happened Matt would just drive on by. He had been to the city many times and knew most of the streets and side streets off by heart. He knew streets and side streets in a great number of cities all over the world. It was one of his tricks. For some reason, he could read city roadmaps and retain the street and highway names and then recognize these same streets upon visiting that city. A crazy mind game but one that had come in handy on more than one occasion. He would use that intimate knowledge of the labyrinth of twisting and turning streets now to follow the men on a side street for a couple of blocks and then rejoin back up, keeping his distance and every once in a while hanging out behind some large truck just in case the crew came to their senses and started looking for a tail. At this point, he could just be someone traveling in the same direction but he had learned not to take any chances.

They had not been inside the city limits for more than fifteen minutes when the poachers turned down one of the streets that was barely out of the residential properties, so even though there were some low rise apartment complexes, there were also some industrial buildings. Low one level corrugated steel roofs that kept the heat and the heavy rain off of everything from the storage of Casava, an elite food source in West Africa, to hundreds of African drums waiting to be sold to tourists.

The street was not in the best neighborhood. If something went wrong here Matt could be sure that there would be no cry for help from any bystander or local citizen. From a couple of streets back he observed the poachers turn into one of the many steel buildings that lined the way. He was careful to make sure that as the truck turned he was looking the other way as if to make a turn in the opposite direction. As he passed the entrance to the building, he looked neither one way nor the other but through his peripheral, he saw that there was no gate or fence and most of the building stood open along one side. The heat of the day would make the inside of a completely enclosed steel building like an oven. Ok if you're drying fruit but not good if you're a human being trying not to die of heat stroke.

It was perfect. He would be able to gain access to whatever was going on without having to break in. The openness of the place would make it very difficult to keep from being seen but he would cross that bridge when he got to it.

He parked the scooter on the street half a block down from the warehouse between two old wagons looking discarded on the street. There was a good probability that it might get stolen if he didn't chain the wheels but he couldn't take the chance if he needed to get away in a hurry.

There was no one guarding the building that he could see as he approached from the side that had walls. One could never be too careful and he kept a keen eye out for any quick movement. As he scuttled around the corner of the structure he could see that the entire length of the place was open to the environment. This side was crammed with barrels three high. They looked like oil barrels but there was no hint of the heavy diesel odor that came with that much crude so he assumed it was some other goods like dates or Cava. Whatever was in them would provide perfect cover for him to explore further.

He kept low and skirted around the end of the row. A line of wooden skids stacked six to eight high left a continuous isle between the barrels and the rest of the interior. Matt used these to work his way toward the middle where he could hear the sound of male voices talking. It sounded like an argument or some serious negotiations. Someone wasn't happy. A good sign. It might keep whoever was involved focused on anything but an intruder.

As Matt neared the voices got louder. From a vantage point just behind some shipping boxes, he could see that a single hooded light hung from a long cord. It sprayed a jaundiced light over a group of men sitting around a large wooden spool. The type typically used to hold long lengths of steel cable. This one was turned on end and held the two great tusks recently ripped from the old elephant left to rot at the oasis. Over them, the four poachers were arguing with two others, likely the buyers. Matt could see the sweat rolling down the faces of the all six so he assumed that the negotiations were not going so good.

It was not really uncommon in this part of the world for a settled priced to be renegotiated upon delivery of the sale item. It was just the way it was. If you thought the Asians could haggle well you never ran up against an African who was trying to make or get a deal.

Matt understood most of what was being said. The

men spoke in broken English and only broke into their native tongue when things got heated. Even then he understood some of the dialects and got enough of the conversation to fill in the blanks.

It turned out that the poachers had made this run before and had assumed that the price for the ivory would be the same as their last visit. The buyers, on the other hand, had gotten wind of the kill and knew that they had taken down a famous herd member. They believed that because the elephant in question was more than just another member of the pack and an esteemed leader that there would be more of an outcry for justice. That would make their job more hazardous and so would cost them more money to transport and sell the goods without being caught. More risk, less gain. That meant that the gain part would be coming out of the poacher's side of things. Something the four men who had traveled for days and taken the risk of cutting the old female down did not see as their fault.

Matt settled in. He would wait to see if the negotiations came to a mutual conclusion and then take up where the poachers left off following the new owners to their hand over point.

After another ten minutes of heated discussion, the two warring parties met half way. The two middlemen handed over a small duffle bag to the four men from the truck and each lifted one of the heavy tusks to their shoulder. A pretty good feat because judging by the size of these tusks, they were easily in the one hundred and seventy-five-pound range. They would raise quite a bit of money if successfully brought to market.

The four poachers had turned and were heading right at Matt. They must have parked at the back of the building where their vehicle was hidden amongst the trash and discarded machine parts from the many inhabitants and businesses the structure had housed over the years.

Mat knew better than to run. He stayed as still as a church mouse as the first three men passed his position. He was holding his breath but just as the last man passed his hiding place he turned for some reason to yell back at the two carrying the tusks away. As he did, the words caught in his throat. He spotted Matt, tucked up close to the packing crates and started to bring his gun to bear with a quick flip of it off his shoulders.

Matt shot him before the weapon even got level. He wouldn't be so lucky with the others. A stream of fire tore the tops of the boxes above his head. As a cover, the thin wood and cardboard construction of the packing crates was not the best for a gunfight but

Matt had the fact that the men had never had to fire their weapons in self-defense before on his side. They were poachers after all praying on those who could not see or defend against them. Their aim was terrible and they had no idea of what they were doing when it came to combat, situation defense or assault.

Matt knew both. He heard the first clip empty and bolted for the cover of the row of skids. Another line of defense that wouldn't create much cover but he would be one step further away from his attackers and on to the safety of the lines of barrels that stood between him and his escape.

The next round of bullets was about as accurate as the last. They were even further away from his position and he could tell that the men were running for their vehicle while they sprayed the general area trying to flee. All they succeeded in doing was to open a few dozen holes in the barrels that lined the outer wall.

As the next volley from the fleeing men ended Matt sprinted to the end of the barrels and around the far end. His path was clear and he was just in time to catch a glimpse of a black Ford cargo van high tailing it from the front of the building. That would be his buyers.

Not all was lost but as he passed the last few barrels he could smell the fluid that was seeping from the ruptures the bullets had made in their sides. It was either paint thinner or nail polish remover, he wasn't sure but he knew just from the way it made his eyes water that it was flammable. He wondered if he could make his scooter and away before a pack of matches would light. Never know unless you try he thought. Pulling a pack of matches from his pocket, Matt pulled one from the row inside, lit it and then re-inserted it back end first. That would work like a wick. The timing was uncertain but if the match burnt all the way down to the rest of the sulfur heads inside the pack, he would have about Fifteen seconds to get away.

He lay the match pack down just beside an expanding line of fluid from the drums and ran.

THE CURVE

Matt's time at the shelter as an inmate didn't last long. Ethan had procured him a well-paid position with the city as one of its lifeguards. Ethan still retained a position with the city as a supervisor for the parks and recreation division. He had started his own dojo many years ago and while busy with the two jobs. Still kept his commitment to the shelter to train those interested for free every morning between the hours of ten and eleven. It wasn't just a commitment to the shelter but one to his wife who he knew would be more than disappointed in him if he didn't keep his promise not only to the drop-in center but to the community as well. Besides he really enjoyed helping the homeless and helpless. Sometimes when he was trying to teach those who came from backgrounds of privilege they came with their own set of rules. Most were looking to gain a skill that would help them revenge themselves on some other person who had either humiliated them or taken something from them. They came thinking that a knowledge of Karate would bring back their respect or would make them able to beat the offending party physically so they could get their property back.

The other group came because they thought it was cool to say they knew Karate or were studying

Karate. They soon either dropped out or became disinterested when they discovered the depth of the commitment it took to become good at the art. Most would never be better than good and few if any would ever be great.

Matthew Buxton, on the other hand, was an anomaly. He came to Karate with no expectations and an innate understanding of the grounding force that drove the form. Once he had mastered the simple basics it was almost like he had been taught the different styles before. He only had to be shown anything once to understand the move and its meaning. He would practice the move until he could perform it flawlessly and then incorporate it into any number of Kata's. It was uncanny. Ethan knew that he would have to take the young man under his wing. He was special even though he might not know it now. Matthew Buxton had something that Ethan had never seen. The ability to move through situations without emotion. To analyze and determine an outcome of his choosing projecting himself into the future and seeing the end result of his decisions before they happened. How he did it Ethan did not know. For that matter, Matthew didn't really know either. The two had sat over coffee many times after a particularly strenuous workout and Ethan would ask Matt how he had known what move he was going to make next and Matt would invariably say the same thing. He just knew. Not the answer Ethan was looking for but Matt didn't fully understand the ability himself and it would be many years before he would truly be able to control it. For the time being, it was a gift and one that would serve Matt well as he moved from the foundation that Ethan had laid for him through his training at the shelter to the private sessions in Ethan's own dojo and beyond. Even more so as Matt made his way overseas to study Karate with Japanese masters, then as a Navy Seal and far beyond even that security level to become a rogue silent operative, working as the most secret asset of American intelligence tasked to bring down the world's most elusive terrorists and criminal minds.

~

Matt's learning curve could be defined as miraculous. Even the old masters he studied with, in Okinawa, Japan would not understand his particular ability. When he joined the Navy after returning to America, they were quick to recognize his abilities and were astounded at his situational expertise and understanding of battle scenarios even while under duress. It wasn't long before the Navy Seals had themselves a poster boy. Matt was brought in on almost every difficult mission from high seas piracy and high jacking to hostage recovery and troop deployment missions in the Middle East. He was uncanny at spotting the flaw in the plan or the weak link in the enemy's armor, something that didn't go un-noticed by special ops and the grey world of the CIA.

After his second tour with the Seals, Matt was called to a clandestine meeting. He was escorted to the USS Ronald Reagan where he met with a select group of government officials, Navy Colonels, and CIA clandestine special agents. He spent five days aboard ship while the assembled team set forth a proposal to him that would culminate his years of training both in the Martial arts and in the Navy Seals as well. He would still undergo another full year of intense scrutiny while he was prepared for missions yet to be determined but critical to the safety and well-being of the United States and North America as a whole. If Matt accepted the proposal, he would be forever on his own. If found out in the course of any of his missions, he would be deemed rogue and hung out to dry. No one would take responsibility for him or his actions and he would be left to accept his fate.

None of these things mattered to Matt. He had been in a precarious position since the day he joined the forces. Even his mother and father thought he still worked for the City of Chicago. He wondered why they never asked to come and see him given they only lived a few hours away by car but he would then remember that he was the only one he knew who had ever left Maddison and never gone back. They were probably standing by the front window right now expecting to see him come ambling up the road to say hi. He was up for the adventure. He had few friends. His work and training had kept him pretty much alone. He had a couple of Seal buddies but he knew not to get to close there either. They had laid out the plan and it all looked good to him. He would do what his country asked of him.

~

Once the US started to track terrorism by tracking and hacking the money lines that funded many of the radical group's hell-bent on taking over the world, they also discovered that they weren't the only ones to use illegal money laundering and offshore accounts buried in miles of cyberspace and red tape to fund their hair brained ideas. There were literally thousands of criminal and legit businesses alike hiding, moving and exchanging huge sums of money in extraordinary ways. These were called streaming currencies. A great amount of the money trading hands ended up in those of the various terrorist organizations around the world. Taliban, Isis, Al-Qaeda, Islamic State, even the Revolutionary Armed Forces of Colombia needed funding and there were others. Their efforts to sustain their overhead and to compete with all the other burgeoning organizations kept them busy thinking up easier and more illegal ways to generate cash flow. It was the acts of these businesses, elephant and rhino poaching, human trafficking, drugs and the flow of illegal funds through the internet that Matt's new friends were interested in tracking. Letting their acts of violence and the money lead him to their leaders and strongholds throughout the world. Their own need to feed would be their ultimate downfall. But first, they had to be found and to that, the trail of money and the commission of gaining that money would be the starting point.

~

For a long time, the US government knew that the illegal sale of ivory was one of the most prolific sources of income for a number of terrorist organizations. The two biggest consumers of illegal ivory in the world? The US and China. Thousands of elephant lost their lives every year to poaching and tons of ivory tusks made their way into American and Chinese hands in exchange for money that eventually ended up in the hands of terrorist organizations around the world.

It is estimated that one hundred elephants are poached every day in the pursuit of their ivory tusks. At that rate, elephants could be extinct in under ten years.

Matt's first assignment would be to find and control those who would use the illegal trade of ivory to support terrorism. The task at hand would be an ongoing protocol that would remain in place until the sources were found out and dried up.

T. U. S. C.

Taskforce to Uncover Systems of Cabal.

It was a lengthy acronym but an appropriate one. What the title didn't elude to was this was to be accomplished by any means possible. That meant Matt. That also meant that Matt could use any resource at his or the government's disposal. He could also use any resource that he could procure. Basically, he had carte blanche to do whatever it took to accomplish his missions and to pinch off the flow of money funding those who would do the US harm. No questions asked.

Matt actually likes the idea. He wasn't the least bit worried about the consequences. He had basically been doing the exact same thing for the Navy Seals except under the restrictions of the Geneva Convention. Now he would be free to use his unusual skill set to its utmost potential. His induction to the program would start immediately and he would be in the field and undercover following that.

There was an urgency to find a way to control the free-flowing black market in illegal ivory and to stem the cash streaming to those bent on forcing their will on the rest of the globe. What the committee did not know was that Matt was not a cold-blooded killer for hire. He had been taught many of the ancient beliefs of the Samurai and had studied the teachings of bushido especially the rules of rectitude, courage, and mercy. Not that he couldn't do what needed to be done to accomplish his mission but he would never take a life or destroy property just for the sake of it. His old mentor and friend had taught him well, so even as his skill as fighter grew so did his sense of purpose and understanding of right and wrong.

THE BIG BOOM

The matchbook Matt had slipped into the expanding line of fluid emanating from the bullet scared barrels didn't work exactly as planned. Probably a good thing for Matt.

The initial set up did go off as he had hoped. The ignition match burned down to the rest of the book and set off the matches igniting the river of fluid they were placed in. This was where the processed slowed down.

Matt had assumed that the matchbook would give him at least a fifteen second lead on the drums going up in smoke he also knew that the flame would ignite the draining fluid but since he had no idea of what the fluid was he could only make an estimate as to how long it would take for the bigger drums to start going off. Luck was with him. He had gotten his scooter going and had seen the buyers hauling ass up a side street and away from the warehouse where he had just left a dead elephant poacher. He was on the far side of an adjacent building and heading after the buyers when the barrels of fluid finally took off. It had taken almost a full minute for the first of the oil drums to go. That one barrel almost simultaneously ignited the remaining three hundred.

The concussion from the explosion would have evaporated Matt but for the building that separated him from the warehouse. As it was glass from its windows rained down on him with the impetus of rock salt from a shotgun. What saved him was the force of the building itself exploding outward. The shock wave from the barrels pushed him and his scooter across the street at almost a ninety-degree angle into an adjoining side street at a velocity almost equal to the wave. The ecclesiastic blast that followed the explosion was intense, melting the tires on Matt's scooter. He could feel the heat penetrating his clothing and searing his skin where it was exposed as he held on and tried to maintain his balance down the street he had been ejected into.

The three poachers that had fired on Matt back in the warehouse weren't so lucky or maybe they were.

Because they had parked at the back of the building their getaway was hampered by various discarded pieces of machinery and used cars. The few small turns it took to negotiate the track from where they had parked to the street were their undoing. They were essentially in direct line of fire when the barrels exploded.

If caught the poachers would have been given long prison terms, a fate worse than death in an African prison. Even hardened criminals had a code when it came to the countries declining wildlife and a known poacher would be treated to tortures that only men with twenty-four hours a day to think of the most disgusting and degrading things to do a human could deploy. As it turned out these three would not have to endure any of that. In fact, the only thing left of the three men and their vehicle was the smoking hulk of the four by four itself. The men had been cremated.

Matt, still in the thralls of the heat wave, was losing consciousness. The intensity of the heat was making it hard to breathe and the combined effects on his skin, hearing, and lungs was not good. The last thing he remembered before he blacked out was seeing an open doorway in the rows of adobe buildings along the street and pointing the still speeding scooter in that direction.

~

Not many were aware of the Satellite system put in place by the US government in 1959 to monitor compliance with the 1963 Test Ban Treaty by the Soviet Union. The program lasted for twenty-six years. Far less knew of the special commission to use part of those satellite's systems to monitor earth for signs of aggression from countries unfriendly to the USA by continuously monitoring those rogue nations for signs of missile launch.

  When that system was shut down in 1984, it was replaced with a program of the U. S. Air Force called the Defense Support Program. This program is currently used by the U.S. as an early warning system. These satellites detect spacecraft or missile launches and nuclear explosions using sensors that detect the infrared emissions from those heat sources. With the launch of the new system came an upgrade for the special commission watching aggressive nations. These satellite's, in geosynchronous orbit, use an infrared sensor operating through a wide-angled Schmidt camera and spin so the sensor array in the focal plane scans the earth six times every minute. The special commission known as TUSC had full executive permission to take over these cameras and focus them on any event that could potentially create risk for America or any of its NATO friends. They could do this with complete secrecy and impunity without notice while at the same time avoiding having to immediately notify NORAD or USSTRATCOM.

  The explosion at the warehouse in Berthoud was large enough that it caught the attention of the infrared scanner aboard one of the twenty-three satellites That video feed had been played back thirty times before it was decided that it was, in fact, just a large explosion. Big by any standard but not a missile launch nor a bomb test. What was disconcerting to a couple of those in the viewing room was that they were the only ones aware that their operative was in the field specifically in Berthoud. His last communication had come from his anchor position inside the city limits. This explosion was close enough to that to cause concern. They could only wait to hear from him. Their organization was so secret that they were the only two who knew even the smallest amount of info regarding ongoing actions involving the single man operation know as TUSC and they did not know who it was that answered the phone when they called or if that person called them. That person was so secluded that they got a different phone number every day on a text and if they tried to call yesterday's number back, even if it was immediately after they received that text, it was out of service. Even at that, they did not know when there was a mission or if their man was in the field. There was only the one above them that controlled the funding, allocation of assets and implementation regarding every insurgency. Their job was to report. Nothing else. This was something that needed to be reported.

~

Matt woke with a huge buzzing in his ears. Like wasps had made papier mache nests deep down in his ear canals and were agitatedly going about their day. He realized he was face down on a bed. The mattress smelled of unwashed bodies and the pillow was rank with the odor of many garlic filled baba ghanoush breathed into its spongy depths.

When he tried to move, the pain in his back almost made him pass out again. The room was dark and Matt could sense more than see that it was night. He remembered the explosion and trying to outrun the heat wave. He could see his dash for the open door in his mind but he could not recollect if he made it through or if this was some kind of stinky hell he had been left in after death. He tried to move once more and the pain now resonated down his back and into his legs. He was pretty sure he was still alive. There was no way that much pain could be inflicted in any kind of hell other than on earth.

As he became more aware of his surroundings and as his head became clearer, Matt understood that those he was pursuing had gotten away. That was a huge letdown. This would be the first time he had failed to complete his mission. That, more than anything else got him through the pain of sitting up and trying to stand.

He tried to get to his feet but the darkness was disorienting. Where was the door, if there was one at all?

His question was, as if by magic, immediately answered as a door opened and flooded the room with a soft candlelight that emanated from the room beyond.

"I would not try to go too far if I were you sir." A soft male voice commented. Not in a demanding "you're my prisoner" way but more in a "I found a hurt bunny and I'm going to keep him" way. The bunny part might have been his addled brain's way of saying he was probably safe but still, the thought was a little creepy.

"You were very lucky to have escaped the firestorm. You must be an angel. Either that or the flames have blasted your skin white"

Matt tried his voice. He could feel the air start to wind its way around his vocal cords as it made its attempt at speech but his first word came out like he was hacking up a bone.

"Ach." He said and then started to laugh. That was bad. Just the little movement the laughter brought on tore through his back like a lightning bolt so he quit that pretty damn quick. His second attempt was a little better. He managed to get out one word.

"Where?"

"The silhouette in the doorway seemed to understand.

"You came crashing through my doorway on your bike just as I was on my way to see what had assaulted the air with such a boom and shook the ground like an earthquake."

"What happened to me?" Matt was finding his voice however it was still hoarse and scratchy.

"I am not sure" the stranger answered "but you are one lucky bugger I must say. I have been outside and there's very little that was not burned by the boom. It is only fortunate that everyone was inside during the mid-day sun."

Matt was thankful that it appeared no innocent had been affected by his blowing up of the warehouse.

"Where am I? Matt inquired. "I feel like I was hit by a ten-ton fireball."

"Yes, when you so loudly announced yourself at our door you were literally smoking. Your back seems to have taken quite a burn and there are still some glass shards I think in your back. We tried to take as many out as possible while you were unconscious but some are in pretty deep. We do not have a lot of things so you will need to get to a doctor to look after your burns. We used a salve that is made from gum bark. It is all we have but we use it for many things including burns. I am sorry we can do no more for you."

"You have done more than I could have hoped for," Matt said. "I am in your debt. Did my scooter survive?"

"I am truly sorry but your two-wheeled cow did not survive the storm.

Matt would have laughed at that but he recalled the pain that ensued the last time he gave in to laughter and refrained.

Matt made the effort to gain his feet. He could hear the sound of police and fire sirens in multitude.

"How long have I been here? Matt asked.

"About six hours." His host responded.

"I must go. Can you tell me your name so I may thank you for your kindness and if you will tell me the name of the street that will be the last thing I will ask of you."

"My name is Abdalla and there is no need for thanks. You will have to get yourself looked at to make sure the burns on your back do not get infected. This street has no name but it lies to the east of a large green space that will take you to the highway on the other side"

As Matt stood the walls suddenly closed in. He felt like he was about to pass out and the pain in his back was excruciating. Abdalla grabbed him as he staggered forward.

"Thank you, Abdalla," Matt breathed out. He could not stay. In this part of the city, one could be as inconspicuous as needed for the most part but the explosion that Matt had set off was far too big to be left unattended and uninvestigated. There would soon be police going door to door looking for answers or perpetrators. He had a rough idea of where the green space was that Abdalla had mentioned and he had a good idea of where it would come out. It was as good as he was going to get. His trusted scooter was down. Both tires had melted with the heat and were flat.

He would have to get out of the area on foot. If he made it to the highway we could hire a car but he needed to look at himself in a mirror to assess whether he was able to pass himself off as just another body on the road or if he looked to beat up and would draw attention to his condition.

He asked Abdalla if he had a washroom. Many people in this part of Cameroon had what passed as a washroom, a tiny area set aside with either a sink and running water or a washstand of some sort with a bowl or pitcher of water for washing both body and food. There was more than likely no toilet. It would be down the street in a community outhouse.

His continence in the small mirror hanging against the adobe wall was little consolation. While his face looked reasonably unscathed a slight turn to the right revealed another story. Starting from his head down he was a mess. His hair, at least the part that had stuck out below his ball hat was gone. Right down to a nasty looking pink blister. The rest of his back, which must have taken the brunt of the blast was charred and pockmarked with incisions left by flying glass on the way in or by Abdalla's attempt to take pieces out.

"Not so nice." Abdalla postulated.

"I will assume by the look of my back that I have no shirt?"

"I am afraid not but I have one of my work shirts that I think will fit. My wife always buys them extra big so I will stay cool."

"Thank you, Abdalla," Matt said taking the man's hand. "I will replace whatever I take."

"Go with God and do not worry about a shirt."

They returned to the room where Matt had first awoken, and Abdalla picked a clean white shirt and his badly singed CO-OP ball hat off the end of the bed.

It fit but barely. Matt would have to roll up the sleeves and tuck it into his pants so no one would notice its shortcomings.

As he exited the door Matt turned to the cool safety of the small dwelling. Abdalla, standing in the door, made a hitch-hiking motion with his thumb to the right. Matt realized he was getting directions and headed off down the street in that direction.

Under different circumstances, Matt would have been walking at a very brisk pace if not running but even the act of putting one foot in front of the other sent shivers of pain up and down his back and that kept him to a very leisurely pace. Probably a good thing. There was no one else on the street. A running man would have brought undue attention to himself. He would have to keep to the dark side of the street and use the shadows as cover.

The buildings on the street looked remarkably unscathed by the blast that had leveled the warehouse and ripped up his back but anything that had been parked or left out in the open was pretty seared and anything made of plastic or rubber was

97

flat out melted.

Luckily the walk along the open road didn't last long and went unnoticed by anyone that Matt could see. The sirens sounded like they were a few blocks over and he hoped they stayed there until he could get a good way into the grove that separated this community with its neighbor to the east.

~

The instant the poacher had raised his gun in Matt's direction back in the warehouse Matt had simultaneously run a number of situations through his head and patched together a viable plan to rid himself of the poachers and follow the buyers to their destination. He had pre-planned an escape and that plan had included blowing the barrels of flammables. He had miscalculated the size of the explosion but only because he could not tell how volatile their contents were. Even after the cans had been riddled with bullets it was still very hard to determine what the fluid was. Probably paint thinner judging by the size of the explosion.

Now as he made his way into the dense foliage at the end of the street his mind instantly recalled the size of the grove from topographical maps he had studied earlier in the day. He then estimated time to cross and time to the highway through the populated area that lay just on the other side. He also took into account his condition and factored that in to determine whether or not he could successfully get back to his safe house before he lost consciousness again.

Matt never factored in luck when in the field. He always thought two steps ahead and in some scenarios four or five steps ahead.

This time, he got lucky. As he emerged from the dense foliage on the west side of the grove, he came up against a long row of parked cars. Most were throwbacks to the area of the box-shaped Toyota Corolla but they all had four wheels and it didn't take him long to find one with the windows down or more likely it didn't have windows. No matter, Matt was in and had it hotwired almost before the door was shut. Not a light came on or a voice raised in pursuit as he drove off into the night and headed back to his place. He would have to abandon the wreck some distance from his pad but this would get him where he needed to go. He would deal with his injuries and re-assess his mission after he figured out how he was going to heal his back and find new transportation.

THE ESCAPE

The report and video of the explosion in Bertoua had been passed the single step up the ladder to the office. The two who had deemed it necessary to move the explosion up the line did not know who would be the recipient of the information nor did they care. The file was sent through an encrypted email address to God knows where. They were just happy to get it out of their hands.

The laptop screen played the exploding warehouse images over and over. Each time the view zoomed in a few more pixels until he found what he was looking for. Even though the resolution had become grainy with the level of magnification three separate yet united scenarios could be seen as the fireball erupted. The first was an almost instantaneous meltdown of a four-wheel drive vehicle that didn't make it off the warehouse grounds. Its occupants vaporized before they knew what hit them. The second, a black SUV running at full speed, made it far enough up a street that ran away from the blast to put three large buildings between it and the searching fingers of flame only slightly bubbling the paint as it made its escape from ground zero. And third and most important, a tiny scooter, not as lucky as the SUV but magically disappearing into a building two blocks away as it ran out of time to outrun the blast.

TUSC could only conclude it was his man. Now he would just have to wait. If Matt survived he would get in touch. They would keep the satellite trained on the building he went into and they would follow the fleeing SUV and see where it stopped. It was night in Africa so he didn't think they would see Matt leave if he did but they would keep an eye on the place until they heard from him. The next order of business was to watch the footage sent on by the satellite team. It was the escape and eventual rendezvous with the second team in Bertoua of the black SUV.

Team one had driven to another group of warehouses on the other side of the city and after about three hours had changed vehicles and were headed out of town on the N10 highway. There was no doubt in TUSCS mind that they had caught a couple of hours of sleep. Picked up supplies and were now headed to Douala. A port city on the Gulf of Guinea. They would probably transfer the tusks there after breaking them down to manageable pieces. After that, there would be no end to where the ivory could be hidden. African furniture on its way overseas to America could have hollowed out legs on tables or chairs. Crates carrying pottery would have bottoms full of straw and subfloors full of ivory. The list went on. It would be over eight hours before the tusk smugglers would get to Douala. A plan was forming but Matt would have to call in before arrangements could be made. If he wasn't injured, he could catch a couple of hours rest and then get there with enough time to set up a surprise for the smugglers. It was up to Matt now. He would have to get in touch.

~

Matt had dumped the old Corolla about six blocks back from his place. The adrenaline had worn off and it was all he could do to stagger back to his bungalow and pass out on the bed.

He awoke about an hour later. The pain in his back had diminished somewhat, at least to the point that he could sit up without black motes floating before his eyes.

First things first. He made his way into the kitchen and dragged a huge bladder of cold water out of the fridge. His thirst seemed unquenchable. He didn't stop drinking until he could hear the fluid slopping around in his belly when he moved. The cool liquid had brought his core temperature down to a reasonable level and he used an old Japanese mind focusing technique to clear his head. Now he needed to check out the damage to his back. It was still very painful but not like it had been when he first awoke at Abdala's.

A look over his shoulder in the bathroom mirror gave him a better view than the mercury veined glass shard that had passed for a mirror before. He could now see that what he had originally thought was pink and bubbled flesh from heat burns was really more swelling from the multiple incisions caused by flying debris that had impaled him on his getaway. Abdala had removed most of the glass but there were other materials stuck in the skin as well. He would have to have someone get the rest of the pieces out but first a cold shower, something to eat and then he would check in with TUSC and let them know that his target had vanished.

~

The shower worked like magic. He could feel the pull of the multitude of tiny holes in his back but his head was straight and he could function. With a clean shirt and pants, no one would know that a few hours earlier he had almost been blown to bits.

As soon as he was dressed he pulled open a concealed door just under the edge of the bed. It was a tricky thing. The floor was made of indigenous mahogany. The trick was to stand on a certain board then push down on the footer of the bed. The pressure of the bed leg on the adjacent board popped the other open revealing a small safe with a digital fingerprint scanner and number lock. The safe held a few treasures. Passports, money and two guns. One was a Walther PPK that Matt loved. It had been a gift from his friend at the reserve for helping with their battle against poachers. He never used it outside of the firing range. He just didn't want to lose it. The other was a Smith & Wesson 9mm. The perfect weapon for quick access and easily concealed. He put the 9mm in the back of his pants, took a few grand from a stack of hundreds that were hidden under the passports and pocketed a cell phone snuggled into the back of the safe.

Once he had everything situated, he relocked the safe, locked the floorboard back down and pressed the power button on the phone. It came alive slowly. It only had about thirty percent power but he only needed to make one call and then he could recharge the battery.

It only rang once.

"Matt." The voice on the other end sounded matter of fact.

"Yup," Matt replied.

"You had us worried. We caught the explosion on the DSP Satellite system. Thought maybe you were a goner."

"No such luck sir," Matt replied. "Take more than a blast you can see from outer space to put me away." He would have added a sardonic chuckle but he remembered the pain his last attempt at humor brought and refrained. "I need a little help though. Seems I picked up a bit of shrapnel in the process so I could use a doc to do a little cleanup."

TUSC was always amazed at how impervious to personal injury Matt was. It was like he could compartmentalize the pain and deal with it until it subsided.

"Ok, here's what we are going to do," TUSC responded. "Not only did we see the explosion from space but we were able to capture a certain SUV making an escape from the blast area. We are tracing it now and it looks like its heading to Douala. I'm going to have a jet ready for you at the Bertoua airport in three hours. It will take you to Douala. I will make arrangements for your arrival. Take your phone and I will give you an update on our SUV. I will get a medic to fly with you and maybe he can patch you up on the way.

Try not to blow anything else up until you get there. Get some sleep and be at the airport on time."

The line went dead and Matt felt a sense of relief. They had tracked the ivory. He fell face down on the bed and was out in a minute the sounds of the night filtered in through the thin walls of the house but he didn't hear them. He slept the sleep of the almost dead and woke a few hours later to the sound of the morning birds and the barking neighborhood dogs that acted as the roosters of the barrio.

~

A couple of hours sleep didn't really cut it but Matt had to get his ass in gear. The rental car that had been languishing under the tarp at the side of the house had been picked up at the airport so he would have no trouble returning the vehicle even if he was a few days shy of his rental agreement. He was pretty sure the rental company wouldn't have an issue with him leaving an early return especially if he didn't want a refund.

He once again braved the shower which in itself was a torture chamber. The water, which was never heated but always stood at air temperature due to the fact that it came down from the cauldron sitting on the roof, was cold enough to send shock waves through every little incision in his back. It did wake him the hell up though. His next excruciating event came when he tried to remove the tarp from the rental car. Just the act of pulling the heavy canvas and folding it up had brought beads of sweat to his brow and a dampness to his armpits that wasn't because of the usual heat of the African sun.

Finally, the house locked and the tarp stashed away Matt climbed into the rental and turned on the air. As he sat back in the seat he could feel the shirt he wore sinking into the numbered blood droplets oozing from his back. He had anticipated the bleeding and had thrown a light windbreaker into the empty front seat. He should be ok because he wouldn't have to go through the usual indignity of the security check. In this part of the world, it didn't take a lot of money to have an airport security guard and an air traffic controller with a family to feed to look the other way.

Still, he had to get there and he was pretty exhausted. Matt's only hope was that he could maintain an air of normalcy until he got himself on the waiting jet, then he could let his guard down. Until then he would have to find a way to stay alert and act normal. Not an easy thing to do with a back that looked like there had been a return to the whipping post as a punishment for talking out of turn.

The ride to the airport was uneventful. No one except for Abdalla had any idea that he could have been involved in the explosion that had rocked the Bertoua neighborhood the day before. He would leave the car at the hangar and one of the rental agents would pick it up.

It wasn't until he stopped at the gate that led to the private hangars that Matt's Spidey sense started to tingle. The guard, while friendly enough did a very odd thing when Matt presented his passport. He turned his back and held Matt's papers up as if he were trying to get a better look or to shade them from the sun.

This guard shouldn't have given more than a passing glance at his passport.

The man turned around with a big shit eating grin and said.

"Everything looks ok Mr. Buxton. Please go on threw."

Matt knew right then and there that something was up and not a good up. It was obvious that someone had paid the guard a little more money than Matts guys had. More likely they had threatened his family and that was a more powerful incentive than greed.

He waited only moments after leaving the gate and the guard post before ducking below the window level of the car. He had just grabbed the Smith & Wesson 9mm that he had tucked under the front seat when the side window exploded raining glass down on him for the second time in twenty-four hours.

Matt had smelled a setup the second the guard had turned with his papers. Now he knew his instincts were correct. He had to determine where the sniper was situated. If he didn't the jet would never get off the ground. Even if he made it aboard without being shot the sniper could take the plane down at his leisure slowly firing off round after round as the aircraft taxied and then took off down the runway. This wasn't the movies. It was a lot easier to hit something vital on an aircraft than it looked. Especially if you had enough time to take a few well-aimed shots and knew what you were doing.

Matthew steered the car with his left hand while he kept as low to the floor as he possibly could. His fucked up back wasn't doing him any favors and he cursed a couple of times as he tried to remember how far and at what degree the hangars resided on the tarmac.

Another shot took out the windshield. That was interesting. The shooter was basically triangulating his position for Matt. As the car traveled down toward the hangars, Matt was gaining a pretty good insight into the shooter's location. He had deliberately not stood on the gas. He wanted the shooter to think he had been hit by the first round.

Another shot took out the back window. Now Matt had him. He would have to crash the car into the side of one of the corrugated steel hangars so he could get his bearings but at the speed, he was traveling that wouldn't cause any damage. The hard part was getting out of the vehicle without getting shot.

He could hear the whine of jet engines as he slowly let the car travel toward where he imagined the hangars were. He had a pretty good map of their location in his mind and keeping the sound of the idling jet to his left it was only seconds before the broken rental crunched into something solid.

Matt threw the door open on the passenger side the second he heard the impact. His intent was to make the shooter believe that the collision had caused the door to jar open. He hoped that there would be a second or two where his focus would be on the open door looking for someone trying to exit and that would give Matt time enough to assess his surroundings.

The second the door swung out Matt popped his head up for a look. Barely breaking the horizon of the dash he saw that he had indeed hit one of the hangars that populated the private area of the airfield. His brief recon was only a second in its length but a bullet slammed into the door frame of the open door almost simultaneously.

That was all the info that Matt needed. Extrapolating the other shots and adding the obvious trajectory of this last round, Matt knew that he could get out the driver's side of the rental and make it into the hangar without much worry of being hit. The gunman's position was high. Probably atop one of the other hangars. He pushed the door with his foot and eased out the driver's side making sure to give the sniper no possible shot. He hit the ground flat on his belly and used the fact that the shooter couldn't get a clear shot because of the extreme angel his position caused as cover.

He had just landed on the blacktop when a bullet skidded passed his face from underneath the car.

This guy was good. He knew where Matt was and was actually firing under the running edge of the vehicle hoping for a rebound impact.

Matt wasted no time. The second the skip shot zipped passed he bolted for the hangar. He didn't have far to run but his injuries from the day before inhibited his ability to crouch and had weakened him enough that he wasn't really sure he could make it.

Two more shots rang off the steel siding of the

hangar as Matt made his way into the cool shade of the open door.

He had an almost exact position for the shooter and knew that if he could get to the where the gunman was secured he could trap him either on the roof where he had been firing from or as the person tried to get down from their perch to escape.

As he started to move through to the back of the hangar Matt saw movement from his peripheral keeping pace with his egress to the back of the building where Matt was going to try and use the exit to get out and around his assailant who he had determined was on the roof two hangars down. As he passed a workbench full of tools needed to maintain the highly tuned fan blades of the Lear Jets that habited these caves he came to an abrupt stop and waited for the following shadow to emerge from behind a series of crates stacked in rows at the back of the shop.

Matt didn't say a word just waited with his gun pointed to the exact place where he knew his shadow would emerge.

When they did, it was not what he expected. It was a woman. A very blonde woman about five foot eight and blonde hair that hung down almost to her waist. It looked almost Barbie dollish except for the Captain's hat and uniform.

The second she caught sight of Matt and the gun, her hands went up but on the way a finger moved over her lips in a "shhhhh" kind of way. The other hand pointed up to the roof of the hangar.

Matt got it right away. This was the pilot of his jet. Likely as good with a gun as with a one point five million dollar aircraft.

Matt lowered his gun and motioned her to come over. When they were face to face, he could smell her. Not your typical soap and hairspray but some kind of coconut oil and sunscreen thing that was truly inviting.

He couldn't believe that was what he was thinking. Refraining from making one of his usual smart ass comments when under duress, he merely said.

"He's not on this building. He's two down. Do you have a gun?"

Her answer was to pull a pretty nice carbon fiber Glock out of the back of her skirt.

" Well, I guess if you have one of those, you probably know how to use it," Matt whispered.

"Fucking rights." The woman exclaimed.

Matt just stared.

"Ok," Matt said. "I'm going to see if I can draw him out. He's on the roof of two down, at least he was. If he's got himself down to the ground, I'll deal with him but if he's still trying to hold the high ground, I'm going to get inside the building and get a couple of rounds up into the ceiling. The second he pokes his head out, you have to take it off."

She just nodded. Matter of fact like no problem I do this all the time.

Mat was skeptical but he didn't have much choice. Neither one of them was going anywhere without getting rid of the sniper.

~

The backs of the hangars were lined up one after the other. He only had to run down to the one where he thought the shots had emanated and go in the back door. Because of the semicircular shape of the buildings, it would have been impossible for the assailant to get a clear shot off between the buildings without sliding of the curve to the ground.

When he entered, he could see that unlike the one he had just come from this one housed only a single Cessna parked near the back with the engine hood up.

Matt used the body line of the plane to keep

something between him and the other end of the building. He didn't know if the shooter had evacuated the roof or if he was still perched atop the building hoping they would run for the jet, Matt had to act fast. Bribing a guard and paying a gunman to shoot someone was one thing but whoever was behind this couldn't have paid the entire airport to look the other way and there had already been too many gunshots to go unnoticed. There would soon be a swarm of police and armed security all over the place.

Matt quickly surveyed the remaining floor area between the Cessna and the front of the hangar. There was no sign of the person who had been shooting at him. Matt hurried to a spot on the floor below where he thought it most likely that a gunman would position himself to shoot down onto the guard station and the runway.

The three shots made a huge echo in the hangar. Matt could hear the footsteps on the roof as his assailant jumped up at the impact of the bullets. There were only two steps before Matt heard a shot from outside and a heavy thud on the roof. Quickly followed by the sound of something sliding toward the edge and then off landing with an even heavier thud.

He ran to the front exit door and pulled it open gun first he eased his way around the door and out into the open. He spotted the woman in the pilot's uniform two hangars down waving to him. He could hear the sound of sirens now from the main terminal and knew if he wasted any time to investigate, he wouldn't be going anywhere.

He ran to her.

"You got him with one shot?" Matt inquired.

"Ya, I was trying for a body shot but I'm a little rusty. It went right through his forehead."

Matt was amazed at the matter-of-fact tone of her voice but also grateful that she had stopped the shooter.

The jet was still idling and the second the hatch closed, his new found friend took her place in the cockpit and started taxying to the secondary runway that managed the smaller aircraft of the private hangars.

As he turned to the seats, he was met by a man in his early fifties. Graying temples but still a thick curly head of hair. He was quite tall and needed to slouch a bit to accommodate his height in the small eight-seater plane. He had on gray light cotton pants and a white shirt with the sleeves rolled up. He reached out his hand and shook Matts.

Please remove your shirt Matt and lay down here. It's not great surgical conditions but it will do.

Matt didn't ask any questions. He took off his blood-stained shirt, made even more so by his recent adventures and lay down on the makeshift bed positioned across two sets of seats.

There was no audible gasp from the doctor or the person Matt assumed was the doctor. He just opened what looked like an old styled carpet bag and began arranging instruments in neat little rows along the side of the platform that was acting as a bed.

"It looks like you took quite a few shards of glass and lot of other debris. I was told someone removed some of the material for you?" He asked.

"Yea, I was extremely lucky. I don't know what kind of a job he did but I'm pretty sure it wasn't optimal."

"No, there are a couple of these wounds that need stitches and there are other materials embedded in some of the incisions. I am going to give you a sedative. It will make you sleep but not for long. Just enough time for me to do a thorough clean up and make sure none of this will get infected."

117

"Hey, do what you have to do. I could use the rest." Matt replied.

"No worries, I've seen worse.

The sedative worked instantaneously and Matt was out. The doctor took his time stitching some of the wounds, removing small pieces of debris from others and crazy gluing the less intrusive ones closed then wrapping Matt's back and neck with burn blister packs for his burns and gauze to keep infection at bay.

QUICK STUDY

Matt had slammed through belts with Ethan in record time. What would normally have taken an attentive student a minimum of four years, Matt had done in a year and a half. It wasn't that he was in a hurry or that he just did what he needed to attain the next level, Ethan had never seen another student with such perfect form, sometimes after only a few days. It was crazy.

Matt had mastered their particular style and achieved his 1st Dan black belt in record time. Ethan knew that Matt was something special and really had to restrain himself from pushing the boy to become more than just a student. Matt had not only mastered the techniques but he had also studied the meaning and spirit of the art. His demeanor when training and sparing were nothing short of amazing. Nothing could fluster him. Always calm and always able to see two steps ahead of any opponent he faced.

They had become quite close friends in the past year and a half. The difference in age didn't seem to bother Matt and Ethan never detected any sense of superiority in Matt's manner or word.

One night over a couple of beers at a pub not far

119

from Ethan's home, the conversation turned to what Matt might want to do to advance his training now that he had his 1st Dan black belt.

Ethan had taken some minutes to explain to Matt how the art proceeded from the point he was at. Making sure he understood the commitment needed to go forward. His analogy was based on levels of learning. Much like in traditional education a 1st Dan Black Belt would be much like a college Bachelor's degree. It was a stepping stone to be used for further education. The 5th Dan would be "Master" level and could be viewed much like a college Master's degree. 8th-degree black belt was "Grandmaster" and could be equivalent to a doctorate degree.

Matt sat as he always did listening intently. Even with the hubbub of the bar, he didn't lose focus while Ethan explained that if he wanted to pursue the sport any further that he would be happy to make arrangements for him and accompany him to Japan to train with some of the old masters that he had trained with before starting his dojo and working at the drop-in center.

"Where would we be going in Japan?" Matt asked.

Funny, Ethan thought, not how or when it was just a statement of acceptance that he would train with the masters and continue his education in the Martial

Arts.

"Okinawa," Ethan replied. I studied there. I can introduce you to my teacher, Tsuneko Machida, if he thinks you have potential, he will invite you to join his Dojo. You would have to remain there until your training was done."

Matt didn't blink an eye. "Are we going soon?" He asked.

It will be up to you. You will have to make arrangements at the city and give notice at work then we will have to get in contact with Master Tsuneko. I will make some inquiries to see if I can get you work. If I do, it won't be work like you have had here. It could be very labor intensive."

"You mean harder than watching tourists fall in the water at the park and rescuing drunk teenagers from the lake when they realize it's deeper than it looks and they are drunker than they think. Ha! I could use a good long rest from that." Matt replied.

Matt and Ethan sat over a couple more beers and started to formulate a plan to get Matt to Japan. It was exciting stuff. Matt had never been anywhere but Madison and Chicago. He knew there would be lots of hard work in Japan not only if he was accepted into the Dojo but also learning a new language and trying to find a job that would keep him fed. The challenge and the change of scenery sounded like fun.

The two conspirators talked into the night before going their separate ways. Ethan was excited for his student who was following in his own footsteps and Matt at the prospect of high adventure in another land.

~

Over the next couple of weeks, Ethan had been in touch with his old sensei and mentor Master Tsuneko. The old master was very interested in Ethan's student. Though skeptical of the youth's abilities, he could hear the sincerity in Ethan's voice when he spoke of his protégé. He would put Matthew to the test himself if Ethan could get him to Okinawa.

Ethan phone Matt the minute he knew the Master would see them and immediately set to work making the arrangements. Once Matt heard the news he gave the appropriate notices to his employers at the city and his apartment manager, both with the caveat that if they did not get an invitation to go to Japan he would remain on. Matt knew that if Ethan had convinced his old Master to give him an audience, Matt would make sure that he was accepted and would stay as long as it took for him to be taught the art to its highest level.

Ethan got the paperwork in order and made the arrangements to take time off from his job and commitments at the shelter. Then he called Matt.

"Ok, we're going." He said, once Matt had answered.

"That's great," Matt responded. "When will we leave?"

"Three weeks. That's when I have booked the airfare, just need a place to stay in case Master Tsuneko does not have room."

"Ok. I have given my notice to work and to my landlord so I will confirm I am leaving and I'll wait for you to get back to me when you have confirmation on flights and lodging and let me know what I owe."

It was just like Matt, Ethan thought, to be thinking about costs and paying his way. It was one of the things that endeared him to Ethan. The kid was always thinking of the other person before his own needs.

~

Matt had given two weeks' notice at his job with the

city but his landlord had needed a month to find a new tenant for Matthews's apartment. That month seemed like a year. He had sold as many of his possessions as he could comfortably live without and he would leave the bed for the next occupant. He was now focused on the next chapter of his life. A long way from two years ago when he had been a homeless, penniless victim of violence lost in a big city. He could attribute his success to the help and guidance of Ethan Miller who had never tried to steer him in any direction but simply advised and counseled him to make wise choices. Matt knew that his trip to Japan would be another step in his search for who he was and what he wanted to do in the world. He couldn't wait to get started.

DOUALA

Matt came too about twenty minutes from landing in Douala. Just long enough for his resident doctor to flip a premade lunch into the microwave and pop open a can of Pabst Blue Ribbon beer.

"Is this the post-operational lunch you offer to all your patients' doc?" Matt queried.

"Pretty much." The guy quipped back. Matt could see the little smirk on the man's face. "Actually you were a rush call so I had to grab some stuff from the hospital commissary on my way out. You're just lucky I had a couple of cans of beer in my golf bag or you would have had to drink water."

Matt didn't think water would have been all that bad right about then as his mouth was dry as a popcorn fart from the anesthetic but the second the cold beer hit his throat he was dam glad there had been a couple of wayward beers left in the guy's golfing equipment.

The micro rang was indicating whatever his newfound physician friend had put in there was ready for consumption and at this point, Matt was ready to down just about anything.

"Sorry, it's not much but better than nothing." The man said as he handed over a very hot kind of meat on rye bread sandwich.

"Thanks." Mat replied. "I don't think it would matter much what it was. I haven't eaten since some time yesterday and I'm famished. How does my back look?"

"Really pretty good considering you were obviously involved in that huge explosion on the east side yesterday. Most of the wounds are superficial. I only had to stitch four of the impacts and crazy glued about ten. The others were just superficial like nasty slivers. The issue is the burns on your neck and any of the exposed skin. I have placed antibiotic gel pads on these areas but I'm guessing those won't last too long judging by the little encounter you had getting into the airport."

Matt had almost wolfed the entire sandwich down and was looking around for another beer. The doctor had anticipated and was holding out another can of Pabst.

"What's your name?" Matthew asked.

"Jim Riley." The man answered. "At your service."

"So how do you get the great job of patching up

random people who almost involve you in a gunfight and then whisk you away aboard a jet for a few hours to patch up someone you have no idea what they're doing or where they came from?"

"Just lucky I guess," Rick replied.

Just then the warning light and seat belt sign came on confirming what Matt had known by the pressure build up in his ears that they were descending. It would only be a few minutes and they would be landing in Douala. Where to from there was anyone's guess.

"Well, thanks for fixing me up," Matthew said.

"It was easy," Rick replied. I've seen a whole lot worse. I was also told to give you this and take the one you have." He handed over an old flip phone that looked like it came out of the nineties. It was beaten up good but Matt didn't question him. He just put it in his pocket and handed over the other.

Matt buckled in and prepared for landing. As the plane lost altitude and headed for the runway he looked out the window at the port city of Douala and wondered how he would track down the runaway SUV that carried the two things he thought he had lost. The ivory and the men that were bound and bent on profiting from the sale of it.

~

Douala was a huge city, one and a half million people with another one and a half million in its surrounding seven districts. Big enough that a couple of Ivory runners could easily get lost and never found.

Its port was the largest in Central Africa and an easy drive from the international airport.

Matt would have to find his escaped ivory traffickers before they made the port. If not there were just too many places for them to hide once they made the labyrinth of shipping containers, warehouses, and outbuildings that made up the huge harbor area. If he lost them here, there were any number of vessels leaving for port unknown and any number of ways to smuggle the ivory aboard any one of them.

Matt didn't want to apprehend the men that he had seen at the transfer in Bertoua. He only wanted to find the next link in the chain that would ultimately lead him to those who benefitted from the sale of the tusks.

If, however, an opportunity presented itself for him to take the money the two would get for the sale of the ivory here. He would be more than happy to relieve them of it. Dead or alive.

~

The aircraft touched down and quickly taxied to a private area northeast of the terminal. Matt could see an old Toyota 4 Runner waiting on the edge of the parking lot.

As the plane came to a halt Matt unbuckled and turned to thank the man who had stitched him up.

"Thanks for putting me back together," Matt said as he extended his hand.

"My pleasure." He replied. "You might want to thank the woman up front. I think she had more of an influence on getting you fixed up than I did."

"Yea, you have a point. What's her name?'

"Beats me." The doctor shrugged. "I don't ask and I don't tell. Once you're off this plane I go back home and act like I just had a long day on the golf course."

"Ok, well, thanks again," Matt said.

Matt turned to the door as the woman who had aided in his escape from the Bertoua airfield emerged from the cockpit.

129

"Thanks for flying with us Mr. Buxton." She said with a beautiful smile.

Now that Matt had some sleep and a bit of food not to mention the two beers that had gone straight to his head, he could see that not only was the woman beautiful but she must also have some mad skills to be able to fly a jet without a co-pilot and handle a gun the way she had back at the hangars.

Matt didn't let any of his thoughts show on his face but as he raised his hand to shake hers he said.

"Yes indeed. It was quite fun. Thanks for your help back in Bertoua. If there is anything I can do for you. Please try to find me."

"Oh, I think our paths will cross again Mr. Buxton. In fact, I know they will."

She said it with such assurance that Matt almost asked her how but he saw the twinkle in her eye and how her smile had changed just enough to tell him that he should leave it at that.

He wasn't on the ground for thirty seconds when he heard the turbines winding back up as the jet started to taxi back out to the runway.

Man, Matt thought that was a hell of a ride. The last twenty-four hours had really taken it out of him and even though he had regained some of his energy while resting on the plane he could feel the recent stitch job tugging at his back and the gel pads meant to help keep infection out of his burns were dripping down between his skin and the back of his shirt making it cling to him and rubbing his blisters to the point of bursting.

The door to the Toyota sitting at the side of the field opened and a short African man stood out and waved him over.

Matt reached around to make sure his gun was tucked neatly into the back of his pants. It was the first thing he had done after placing the money belt he had brought from his place in Bertoua back around his waist before deplaning.

Matt knew that no matter what, as long as you had money and a gun you could accomplish just about anything.

Matt needn't have worried about his driver. The man had been given instructions and to him, Matt was just another businessman who needed to be dropped off at the harbor.

"Where we off to?" Matt inquired once he was settled in the back seat.

" Harbor." A one-word reply that meant the guy

behind the wheel did not speak English or had been told to keep his mouth shut.

The ride to the harbor was uneventful. The road was one of the better paved Matt had been on in Africa and the driver didn't say a word. He had time to go over the last twenty-four hours and analyze what had happened. After a five minute review, he came to the conclusion that there was nothing he could have done to minimize the explosion at the open air warehouse. He was just pissed at losing his target and getting himself injured.

He was just about to ask the driver how much longer when the phone that Doctor Jim had given him began to ring. When he answered a voice on the other end said.

"Don't say a word, just listen." That was fine with Matt.

We're tracking the two that got away after the blast in Bertoua. They are about forty-five minutes behind you and we think they will be heading for the harbor. If they take a side track I will call. Otherwise, you will have to figure out where they are going and a way to find where the cargo goes from there. Once you make contact with your party throw the phone away. The Maritime Museum second floor balcony looks like a good place to get some culture and waist forty minutes.

The line went dead just as the driver pulled into the parking lot of the Sabina and Maritime Museum.

The driver never looked back as Matt handed him some cash. It was American dollars and he was pretty sure enough of them to keep the driver from wondering who his fair had been.

Douala Maritime Museum was a crazy looking multicolored two-story building that housed everything from the story of ancient African wayfarers to modern day shipping in Cameroon. It's modern style and bright colors made it stand out like a sore thumb amongst the ramshackle drudgery of the harbor.

Matt walked through the main level of the Museum with very little interest in its displayed treasures. He stopped only twice on his way to the huge stairwell that led to the second floor, not because he was interested in what rotting piece of history was on display but merely to keep attention from himself as he sought to gain the upper level where he could recon the road below.

The second level was much like the first. Its shining floors cluttered with maritime displays, mostly from the era of steam and coal where the lower level that had been an homage to the past. There reed boats built on sandy beaches launched into raging seas in

133

hopes of finding enough fish to feed a small local community sat draped with aged nets woven from bamboo and knitted together with needles made of palmetto wood.

The balcony he had seen from the parking lot was deserted but for a few plastic tables and chairs. It looked like a place for visitors to sit and enjoy a snack purchased from the vending machines found on the main floor or a coffee while discussing the tragic stories of sailors lost, stories that are a mainstay of any worthwhile maritime museum.

Matt picked a light blue plastic chair and pulled it close to the railing. While pretended to read through some printed material he had snapped up from one of the displays he kept an eye on the road below. It was the same road he had taken from the airport and it was essentially the same road that the black SUV had taken from Bertoua, the N3. The two men would either stay on point or keep with the highway which bypassed the harbor.

The air was heavy with the smells of the shipyard. Creosote mixed with diesel and the ever-present rot of saltwater, dead fish and seagull shit. It was almost overpowering.

As he sat Matt cleared his head and did a quick assessment of how he felt. Except for the uncomfortable pulling that was a result of however many stitches he had been given, he didn't really feel that bad. The bit of food Doctor Jim had provided had been just enough to get his blood sugar going and the two beers had gone a long way to changing his mood.

All in all a rough twenty-four hours but he'd felt worse.

While he sat his mind drifted to the pilot of the aircraft he had just left. Who was she? Where did she come from? As far as he knew he was a one-man operation. No one was supposed to know anything about him or his mission. There was to be only one point of contact and both he and Matt had sworn an oath of secrecy. Matt had always operated under the assumption that if he was ever caught or outed that he would be on his own. No one would vouch for him. For that matter, no one was supposed to know who he was or his name. For all his time with T.U.S.C., he had never talked to or had been in contact with anyone who acted in tandem with one of his insurgencies. He had often been amazed at how assets seemed to pop up when needed. Like the jet and the taxi driver at the airport but he had never had another human being stand beside him in a time of need.

He wondered if she had acted on her own or if

she had been ordered to make sure he made that flight. Was she associated with T.U.S.C. or just a "for hire mercenary"? If she was a mercenary she was a pretty damn cute one...

His thought came to an abrupt halt as he caught a glimpse of what might be the vehicle he was waiting for. Three minutes later he was sure. A black SUV. It had taken the cut off to the harbor and was headed straight at him. Matt decided that he would wait in his perch on the balcony of the museum and try and track them as they came past. From his vantage point, the harbor splayed out before him like a giant jigsaw puzzle each piece almost haphazardly fitted into place to make one big picture.

If the men went too deep into the labyrinth Matt would have to find another way to track them down. He watched as the vehicle rolled right past his position and turned left at the next street. Matt made a beeline for the back side of the building. He got there just in time to see the SUV turn down the street directly behind the museum and come to a stop behind some shipping containers parked outside the warehouse there. He watched as the two men he had seen making the trade with the poachers in Bertoua got out and made their way into the building.

"Shit," Matt mumbled under his breath. He'd

already had enough of warehouses for one week. Why couldn't they have found a nice office building or an office area to do their trade?

Probably would look a little suspicious carrying big elephant tusks into an office building but you never knew. Some of these guys weren't too swift.

He was just about to turn and head down to where he had watched the two enter the building when they reappeared. Opening the back of the truck each grabbed what looked like two burlap bags. They were big and heavy and even from Matt's vantage point he could see that the bottoms of the bags were discolored, possibly blood from the tusks where they had been ripped from the elephants face.

So these two were smart enough to cut the tusks into pieces. That would make their transport less obvious but sometimes the receiving party downgraded the tusk because once cut the ivory would be defined by the size of the piece and some customers wanted the ivory to be pristine when delivered.

Matt decided to keep the cell phone instead of tossing it away in some random trash can. He had a feeling he might need it again as he hurried down from the second floor. Keeping a calm pace he circumnavigated the building and made his way into the back lot of the museum.

The lot was populated with many cargo containers and transport trucks. Fences ran down two sides but the back was designated by a row of thick trees. Here some of the growth had been cut out to give access to the street beyond.

Matt used this cover to get right up to the particular container that hid the SUV and the men he had just witnessed carrying what he was pretty sure was poached ivory, to another drop off point on its way to funding terrorists.

He had moved from the shelter of the trees to the side of the container just as he heard a door open and the sound of the two men returning to their truck. It would seem that four bags weren't enough to carry all their ill-gotten load. When he heard the door to the building open and close again he came around the container to inspect the vehicle. If there were more bags in the back he would wait until they had emptied it. If the hatch was closed he would have to find a way into the building.

The back was empty but the hatch was open. That meant one of the men would be back. Matt went back around the other side of the container and waited. The door of the building opened and closed. Then the hatch of the SUV closed.

Matt picked up a piece of discarded cardboard form the ground and ripped a one-inch strip off one end. He poked his head around the side of the box and as the man turned to re-enter the building he snuck up behind him. Stealthy and silent Matt let the door start to swing shut behind his prey and just as it was about to shut he bent down and shoved the cardboard strip under the bottom edge of the closing door.

Matt sprinted back behind the front of the SUV but he knew the trader would have been too preoccupied after such a long drive and having to get back to the negotiations for the sale of the ivory to even notice that the door had not shut completely.

He was right. He gave it enough time to be sure the second man wouldn't come back and then made his way to the door.

Opening it a crack he could see that it led to a hallway. Luckily it was deserted. Easing the door shut behind him, Matt went into serious stealth mode. He slowed his breathing and placed his feet softly as he traversed the hall to where it intersected He listened for the sound of footsteps or anything that would alert him to someone else in the passage beyond but he heard nothing.

He moved into the adjoining hall and pulled the

gun from the back of his waistband. The eyesight on the nose temporarily caught in the band of his underwear and gave him a bit of a wedgie. He almost laughed as he progressed down the hall lined with steel doors each with a different nameplate written in African. He didn't care what language was written on the doors, one of them hid the men he was after and he would not make the same mistake of getting too close again. This time when he found them he would wait for someone else to make the first move.

He didn't have to look too far to discover the whereabouts of the two who had brought the ivory. Just like in Bertoua the exchange was antagonistic. The loud arguing coming from one of the closed doors told Matt everything he needed to know. The men were speaking in Arabic, a language that Matt was familiar with and could speak fluently. They were arguing over the fact that the ivory had been cut into pieces and would now be worth far less than originally agreed upon.

Matt could tell from the different accents that there were three others in the room, besides the two he had been following. That would likely mean that there would soon be an agreement or there would end up being only three in the room. Matt hoped that would not be the outcome. A couple of dead guys at this point would really throw a screw into his plan.

Matt decided to wait outside the door he had just come in. The door opened out and to the left. He would stay hidden and take the two men from behind as they exited the building. He had an ace up his sleeve, a secretive system learned in Japan called kyusho jitsu or pressure point attack to render the men helpless. Too much pressure they would die, just enough they would be unconscious for a long time. He would then pull them behind the rail container that hid their vehicle from the street and take the SUV.

He knew the men he would then be dealing with would not come out the same door as the traders. Matt knew they would have a back way out. If he could disable the first two and then set up camp in the SUV along an adjacent road on the other side of the building he would have a great view of three of the four escape routes the traffickers could take and if he parked in a position that gave him a clear line of site down the opposite side of the building he would be able to catch anyone exiting carrying burlap bags.

The two men came out of the building still arguing about how they had been ripped off and what a shit amount of money they had been paid considering the danger they had escaped in Bertoua. Neither one knew what hit them. With lightning speed, Matt rendered them both unconscious one not even realizing the other had stopped talking before he was out cold as well.

Matt wasted little time with them. It was all he could do to keep back his bile while he pulled them in between the cargo containers. The two of them smelled of sweat and spicy food made unbearable by the long drive in a hot car. He was pretty sure one of them had pissed his pants when he knocked him out too. He checked their pockets and came up with two tightly wound rolls of bills. These he took along with the keys to the SUV. Leaving the two dealers to their fate he drove to the back of the building and parked at the far end. He rolled all the windows down as the atmosphere inside the vehicle, made more rancid by the heat of the day, was exacerbated by the jars of urine in the back seat, the product of two desperate men on a mission. While he waited he pulled open one of the rolls. It was about ten thousand Central African Francs. Not a lot considering the tusks the two men had delivered could bring as much as three hundred thousand or more on the black market but a big chunk of change for these parts.

He didn't have to wait long. He spotted a door open about halfway down the side of the building he had just recently exited. A curious head poked out and scanned up and down the narrow street. With that bit of reconnaissance out of the way, all three walked out the door carrying the burlap bags full of ivory like they had just found a few pounds of potatoes and were on their way home for a feed.

These three were just about as lackadaisical as the group who had originally poached the tusks. They checked up and down but the street was deserted so up with the trunk on the weathered old Mercedes S Sedan and in with the bags.

Matt slid down in the seat as the Mercedes came to a stop at the end of the access road and turned left. He was surprised to see them go that way. He knew from his drive in from the airport that there was nothing in that direction except more harbor buildings, offices and the Wouri River. That meant that the next point of contact was already here in the harbor. These men were the last point of sale in Africa. They would either accompany the ivory out of the country or they would see it onto a ship that would take it to a final point of sale in either America or China. If he was lucky these would be the only two choices to get rid of the poached goods. Both countries even with America's ban on the sale of ivory were responsible for the greater part of illegal ivory sales in the world.

LESSONS LEARNED

Matt had never been on a plane let alone for the fifteen hours it was going to take to get to Japan. For that matter, he had really never done anything sustained for more than four hours and that would have been while training for his 1st Dan Black Belt. To think that he would be confined to a chair bolted down to a tube flying thirty-six thousand feet in the air did give him some pause. What would he do with himself for that long in one place? Sure, he had Ethan to talk to but ever since he could remember he had never been cooped up indoors for more than the eight hours it took to get some sleep.

He needn't have feared. Once they were in the air it was pretty comfortable. The seats, three in the middle and two on either side were soft and the flight was not full. Ethan and Matt were in the middle seats and once the plane was in the air and at altitude, the seatbelt sign came off and a flight attendant came by to let them know that they were welcome to pull up the armrests and stretch out along the length of the three middle seats.

Matt & Ethan had sat together for a while and chatted about what would likely be expected of him if he were accepted into Master Machida's Dojo. The attendants came around and supplied a really

good evening meal and both men took the mini
bottles of red wine offered as part of the menu. If
didn't take Matt long to doze off. He had been
working on short sleep since he sold his bed and
furniture and was relegated to a really lumpy mattress
thrown down on the living room floor in Ethan's
home for the last few days. Ethan had told him that if
he was accepted into Master Machida's Dojo, he
might be given a room at the master's home. If so he
would be sleeping on a traditional Japanese sleeping
mat or futon and though the Japanese had been
using these as mattresses for hundreds of years he
should be prepared for some pretty uncomfortable
sleeping until he got used to it if he ever did.

Matt thought that would be the least of his worries.
He had picked up a book on how to speak some
simple Japanese words and though the actual
meaning and pronunciation looked like they may be
doable he wasn't as confident of how the hierarchy
of status worked. He guessed he would find out
pretty quick if he didn't get it right.

The two men dozed until the landing for fuel in
Hawaii jolted them awake.

Matt stared out the window taking in the beautiful
palm trees and the aqua blue of the ocean. He
unbuckled his seatbelt and got up to stretch his

legs. He wandered up and down the aisles nodding here and there to people who caught his eye as he passed. He asked about flight time to Okinawa from an attendant in the forward galley as he passed and was told they still had ten hours to go. He was already stiff and vowed to get up every hour or so to shake the cramps out.

After returning to his seat and watching Honolulu's beautiful countryside and water fade into the distance he and Ethan talked some more about life in Japan. The flight attendant brought breakfast. Matt had lost touch with time. He felt more like dinner but breakfast was good. He read some of the magazines available in the seat back in front of him and dozed off again for a few hours catching up on the sleep he had lost while living on Ethan's floor.

Awakening from his second nap Matt had only time to go to the bathroom, wash his face and check his bloodshot eyes in the mirror before the captain was calling everyone to buckle up for landing.

Matt, head jammed into the porthole, was amazed at how small the island seemed. Much like Honolulu the runway was pretty much in the ocean. He had slept through the approach in Hawaii so watching the decent out his window he hoped the pilot would get the big aircraft stopped before they plunged into it at the other end. He needn't have worried.

It was surprised at how tropical and humid it was. He was used to the humidity living near a big body of water but this was different. The salty smell of the ocean reminded him of an old fish tank. The humidity was intense. He could feel the sweat running down his armpits and they had only walked from the plane about one hundred feet to the terminal.

Matt waited for the luggage and Ethan rounded up the rental car.

It wasn't much of a drive from the airport to Master Machida's Dojo and home but Ethan having been before took the crowded expressway to the other side of Lake Man and hurriedly got off onto highway 29. The traffic wasn't much better but at least they would get a bit of a sense of the landscape and the culture. Ethan was surprised at how things had changed since he had been to the island. Where once there had been fields still attended by kimono wrapped workers bent to the task of planting rice, now stood modern storefronts or three-story apartment complexes. Here and there as they drove a traditional Japanese Uchi stood guard over the old traditions, huddled behind courtyards of hedge and bonsai tree, the homes hidden rice paper walls and tatami mat floors testament to the old ways passing away faster than Ethan and Matt went by in their new

147

Toyota Camry.

The Master's home stood just outside of Asato about thirty minutes north of the airport. A small town close to the sea that still had some agricultural land worked by families who had endured a thousand years of feudal tyranny and lately the ongoing occupation of the US.

Nestled between two fields of Goya (nigauri, bittermelon) and Fuchiba a medicinal leaf, Master Machida's home & Dojo had stood the test of time. Built in the traditional Edo period its sliding doors and inner courtyards kept time at bay. Clay tiles that had survived the heat of the centuries still held the rain while hording the cool night air keeping the interior moderate throughout all but the hottest afternoons.

Ethan had schooled Matt in the protocol of meeting the Master but he had not prepared him for the man's physical appearance. Ethan had told Matt on the flight that Okinawa was home to some of the oldest people in the world. Some well into their hundreds. It was attributed to a healthy eating regimen and physical labor. That information had not fully explained the little man that shuffled out to meet them at the front door.

He seemed a little more wrinkled than a fridge magnet and stooped to the point of having to crane his neck upward to peer at the two visitors. His traditional rob hung on him like a tent and his geta (woodblock shoes) creaked as he swayed against the wind whipping about the door.

Matt could only wonder at the things someone of his seemingly advanced age would know. He also wondered at how this old man would test him physically. Maybe he would just have to do a few Katas and he would judge him on those.

Boy was he wrong.

~

The introductions made, Matt was informed that he would have a room at the Dojo if he passed his test.

"That's great." Ethan said. "It will save you a lot of money and you will truly get the benefit of living in Master Machida's presence full time."

Matt was grateful that he wouldn't have to figure out living arrangements and the small town was nearby his residence at the Dojo so that would definitely cut down on any travel time he would have living there.

Shoes left at the front door, Matt was shown to his room. Everything Ethan had discussed with him about what he could expect if he lived at the Dojo was the room to a letter. A small sleeping mat on the

149

floor with a raised table at its foot. The table obviously sized for those sitting on the floor. Two earthen saucers on either side of the sleeping mat held the remnants of candles while an image of some long dead relative hung on a single wall. The room was separated from the homes central courtyard by sliding rice paper doors that looked like they wouldn't keep out a windy day let alone a cold seaside night but it was going to be home so Matt deposited his meager belongings and followed Ethan and his new Sensei to a much larger room more central in the house where two other men were already seated at a low table.

As they entered, the men rose and bowed to Master Machida and then to the two newcomers.

The two were also students of the Sensei and would be training with Matt along with a number of others that were under the Sensei's tutelage.

Dinner was a mix of rice with miso soup and other dishes. Fish, pickled vegetables, and vegetables cooked in broth. Matt would find that this traditional style of eating would at first be hard to maintain after his American diet of meat and high fat but he would eventually find that it improved his response time

and after a couple of months he didn't miss his old

diet at all.

~

The next morning sunup was the call to training. The day would start with Master Machida's assessment of Matt's skill and determine if he would be staying to train or on a flight back with Ethan. Ethan would watch the session and assessment but would have no part in the outcome. He was staying on in Japan for a few days to revisit some old haunts and take a break from Chicago before heading back to America.

When he slid the door to his room open Matt saw he was awaited by nine others in the training area which was essentially the middle courtyard of the house. The ground packed down hard as cement with the pounding of hundreds of feet over many years of martial arts training.

Matt stepped into the courtyard and bowed to the Dojo then turned and bowed to the Shomen.

He had scanned the walls looking for the Shomen before he had stepped down from the house proper into the courtyard and had found it high up on a wall at the back of the yard.

The others which included Sensei Machida, Ethan, the two men he had met the night before and six others he assumed were also other students here for training but also to witness his interview.

Matt joined the group and took a place at the bottom or the Shimoza side of the Dojo. This was traditionally the place where junior students sat. It was a sign of respect to those in the room and he briefly caught Ethan's slight affirming nod as he did so.

Matt joined the group as they did their opening warm ups and katas. Then the group was teamed up to spar at one side of the courtyard while Matt was beckoned to the front by Sensei Machida.

"You will be my sparring partner today." The Sensei said.

Matt was not surprised. He had watched the aged Master at dinner and he could see that even though Sensei's appearance was that of an old man he moved with the grace of a jungle cat and there was a certain look in his eye that told of the Master within. One thing for sure Matt would not be fooled by the man's ancient demeanor.

The two men bowed and moved in. The courtyard became eerily silent as the other trainees stopped what they were doing to watch. Having the master teach a foreigner a lesson was always good fun and would be the talk around the dinner table for a month.

Matt did not notice the others, his focus was absolute. The Sensei's gi hid the old man like a giant bag but Matt was dialed in and could feel the air move with the subtle change in balance of his opponent. It telegraphed his plan. Matt knew that Ethan had told the Sensei of his ability, he was also pretty sure he had not told him of his other enhanced senses. The ones where he could foresee an outcome especially when in combat.

As the attacker Sensei Machida would have to strike first. Matt waited. He could almost hear the Master thinking. He realized that the older man would not try a few tentative blows but would string a series of events together in a well-practiced sequence that he had no doubt use hundreds of times to bring an unwary opponent down.

As the attack began, the first punch was not telegraphed to the casual onlooker. It appeared as it was, a lightning strike coming from an odd stance that would have thrown most defenders off. Matt was ready. He had seen the slight shuffle of feet and the un-weighting of the leg in preparation for the strike. As the Master attacked Matt stepped back from each move bringing his opponent along just out of range while he reserved his defense.

153

Ten moves and the Master stopped on the spot. Matt waited. Not out of breath but truly amazed by the old man's agility. He focused himself for the next flurry.

It did not come. Instead, the Master bowed to Matt waited for the returned bow and left the courtyard but not before giving the gaping group of students a good chastising for shucking their chores.

Matt looked at Ethan. Had he done something wrong? Why had the Master left without a word? He walked back to where Ethan was waiting.

"Did I do something wrong?" He asked.

"Hardly," Ethan replied. "In fact, I think you may have just surprised one of the most revered Karate Masters left in the world."

"How so." Matt was confused.

"Well, he pulled those exact same moves on me when I came here to study and I was black and blue for a couple of weeks after. He never even touched you. I'll bet that hasn't happened before."

Mat was shocked. He had really been in the zone but he really hadn't thought about it in the moment, he just reacted to what he saw coming.

Just then, Sensei Machida re-appeared at the main

door that led to the arena. He beckoned the two men to follow him while calling the other students to work harder.

Once inside Matt and Ethan were led to the main dining room where the night before they had sat with Machida's other two students.

They were told to sit and when tea had been poured, Sensei Machida spoke.

Looking directly at Matt he said. "How did you defend yourself against my attack? Did Ethan San tell you of these katas?"

Matt was surprised. "No Master." He replied." Ethan San gave no indication of what to expect."

"Then please enlighten me as to your defense."

"I watched for the subtle changes in your balance and envisioned the movements under your gi through the movement of the cloth. I then developed an image of the attack from start to finish in my mind's eye and with some small variations the attack proved out."

"Thank you. You may go and join the others. One of the older students will get you started in our routines."

Matt bowed as he left the room but thought that if he was headed back out to the yard to start training he must be in.

~

When Matt had left the room Master Machida had a little chuckle. "So my old student has brought me someone who can teach a Master."

"I did not mean any disrespect Sensei. His talent is sometimes easy to see and sometimes mysterious. I brought him to you because I can no longer give him what he needs."

"I don't know if I can either Ethan, he has something I have seen before but only slight glimmers of understanding. This young man has complete control of a sixth sense. It would be a Masters lifetime duty to make sure his talent is not wasted."

"I think you will find that this young man is different. I have never seen him waste anything."

Master Machida bent to his tea. "Then I must take him under my wing and return him to you when he has become who he will be. A great warrior."

Dinner around the table that night was pretty much the same as the night before. The food was vegetarian except for some tempura shrimp and the ever-present tea seemed endless. One thing that was different was the lack of conversation. The night before the other two students were eager to find out about Ethan and Matt. Where did they live? How big was the City? What did they do for work? Tonight they were conspicuous in their silence. They had witnessed the amazing display of control Matt had in the spar with the Master and weren't really sure if they should bring it up.

After dinner, the two men bowed to their host and the other students and made their way to their respective rooms. Ethan would be leaving in the morning and Matt still did not know what his status was at the Dojo. As they walked Matt asked if he had offended the Master. Ethan assured him he had not. In fact, he had greatly impressed the old man. He told Matt that Master Machida was willing to take him in and teach him everything he knew. He would also not have to find a job if he didn't feel the need. The Master would provide him with whatever he needed. It was a great honor to be taken in and taught by a Master of Machida's ranking.

Matt thanked Ethan for all he had done for him and told him he would see him the in the morning.

He would sleep well tonight and be ready for the future to unfold tomorrow with his first day as a full-time student.

THE CONNECTION

The SUV was pretty conspicuous. Covered in light desert sand from the long drive, it stuck out like a sore thumb amongst the reasonably clean city cars.

Matt kept his distance and when the old Mercedes pulled in to a dockside warehouse, he ditched the SUV and set out on foot.

The warehouse was a typical big port structure. Two stories and long with a corrugated roof held up by aged and stained red brick walls. It would be difficult to get inside via the front door but dockside there were numerous skids holding boxes wrapped in cellophane and heavier wooden crates containing palm oil and Cocoa awaiting loading to a freighter. Matt could use these containers and boxes to hide while he sought his traffickers.

He could hear men talking about a hundred feet from where he crouched in the staggering heat and rotting stench of the docks. The noise of the huge crane loading the skids and container to the ship hid his approach as he slinked his way to within a few feet of the conversation. Lying flat on his belly he peered around the base of one of the skids and watched as four men argued about how to hide the

159

hewn tusk in with what looked like a large wooden crate loaded with palm oil and straw packing material. They were definitely going to load the ivory on this ship. Matt turned his head to the ship. USS Algon written in white letters on the side stood out like a beacon against the rusted brown of the hull.

The two bullets that ripped into the wood of the container he was sprawled beside would have taken his head off if he hadn't of looked over at just that precise moment. His reaction was instantaneous. He hit the first crack between two skids of cargo and was off down the dock using the rows of waiting cartage to block his escape. Two more shots splintered up wood very close as he became exposed here and there between the crates. He could also hear the men that he had been watching or at least some of those men in hot pursuit. Their feet making it obvious they were in chase as the creosote beams of the wharf resounded behind him.

Matt was in shape and even though the last few days events had worn him down, he was still faster than a couple of criminals and a dock worker.

He made the SUV and cranked it into a full three-sixty heading for the airport. He reflected on what a good idea it had been to toss the jars of urine out of the back seat before he took up his surveillance. He also felt fortunate that he hadn't abandoned the cell phone he was supposed to dump. It was at least some assurance that he had a contact point or at least a way to make a call if needed.

The number that had wrung him in the cab rang when he pushed the send button.

"Fucking new you wouldn't get rid of the phone when I told you too." The voice on the other end sounded exasperated.

"Well, I missed you." Matt retorted.

"Trouble?" the voice asked.

Matt was just about to answer when the back window blew out and not just in a shy way. The round that took it out also destroyed most of the front window as well.

"Does that answer your question?" Matt yelled back over the wind noise created by the lack of glass.

"Get to the airport. I thought there might be some trouble so I sent the good doctor back on a domestic flight and kept the jet ready and waiting."

"On my way."

Now Matt had only to deal with the cannon fire from whoever was chasing him.

Matt's knowledge of the road he was flying down was limited to what he had gleaned on the trip in. He did want to shake whoever was tailing him before he got to the airport and before local law enforcement got involved.

Matt could see the car behind him but it was still a ways back. One thing for sure it was big. Like an old sixties Caddy or something. It was also carrying a big gun.

Matt pulled the gun he had been carrying out and reaching over the back seat squeezed off a few rounds back through the windowless back seat. Using the rearview mirror to sight he saw a couple of spider webs appear on the oncoming Caddy's windshield.

That might slow them down for a sec but it won't last he thought.

The buildings were starting to thin out and Matt knew that if he got out on the open road without a good jump on the Caddy they would catch him pretty quick. He slammed on the brakes at about seventy miles an hour and careened the SUV into an open side street. The labyrinth of streets worked like a maze. The SUV's smaller wheelbase quickly put some distance between it and the following vehicle but not without rattling of a few parked cars and a few close calls from the shooters firing from behind.

Ten minutes later Matt emerged onto a side road that took him directly back to the highway. He started his run for the airport with a sizable head start but would it be enough?

~

Matt kept an eye on the big black car in the rearview mirror. He calculated that he would have enough time to make the airport but maybe not enough to ditch the SUV and get to the jet without incurring some fire.

It was just about then that something that felt like a tank round ripped through the right-hand roof supports and the glass side windows literally tearing the top right half of the SUV in half and leaving it resting on the top of the door panels.

The resulting explosion made Matt's ears ring and he almost swerved into the ditch before regaining control.

The SUV was pretty funny looking. The roof now slopping off to the right at a thirty-degree angle and spastically swerving down the highway like a drunken sailor.

What the hell could they be firing at him? If he took another round like that it would be over. He was swerving all over the road now trying to give them a more difficult target. The airport was in sight and he still hadn't come up with a plan.

This time the round missed by inches but Matt heard it pass by the driver's side on its way to who knew where. If any other car had been coming the other way it would have been a total wreck. This time he heard the retort of the gun millisecond after he heard the projectile pass. That meant that they were closing the gap. He had better get his act together fast.

His destination was at the far end of the main terminal. Out where the private hangars and runways stored the corporate jets and helicopters with access to the main runway and two smaller lengths of asphalt specifically for smaller aircraft.

It was going to be close. He would have to ditch the SUV outside the fence and make a run for the gate or take a chance climbing the fence before his pursuers caught up.

Anxiously eyeballing the speeding tank behind him Matt was calmly trying to calculate how many seconds he would have to get to the jet. It would depend on how close he left the broken bucket he was in and whether he jumped the fence or made a play for the gate. Either way, it would be excruciatingly close.

He had no sooner decided on a break point when he heard the scream of tires in an impossible attempt to hold on to pavement. He took a quick look in the rear view just in time to see the big black Caddy and its occupants careen to the left and as if the tires had stuck started an incredible barrel roll down the middle of the highway. The right side connected with the pavement first sending the car up into the air as it flipped onto its hood. Then skidding a few feet before repeating the second half of the roll. Over and over it went. Matt saw one of the occupants shoot straight out of a side window and launch twenty feet into the air. He got his eyes back on the road before the guy even came down.

He didn't slow down until he made the manned gate. The shock look on the attendant's face said it all. The SUV was totaled. Still, Matt was having a hard time keeping a smile off his face.

After showing his passport and explaining that he was having some body work done, Matt slipped the guard a fist full of American Twenties. More than the guy would make in a month and drove on.

The jet was right where he had left it and so was the beautiful captain. He parked the SUV in a parking lot alongside one of the corporate hangars. He thought it was pretty funny that there was a space between a new BMW and a pretty fancy looking Harley Davidson. Someone was in for a shock when they came to pick up their vehicles.

Matt bounded up the stairs. "Let's get the hell out of here captain." He said.

"Don't have to tell me twice." He would have had a witty comeback but the .300 Win Mag Sniper Rifle leaning up against the bulkhead as he entered gave him some pause. He had trained on one of these as a SEAL. He was pretty good with it too but what was it doing sitting out in the open like this?

"You been killing bugs while I was gone?" Matt asked.

"Not anymore," she said as she settled into the captain's chair. "I did have a nasty big beetle problem a few minutes back but I took care of it."

Matt was impressed. He realized the reason for his pursuers stock-car esque rollover was because his savior, once again, had been this jet flying, pistol-toting blonde lady. What was even better was she would have had to have fired from inside the aircraft to stay hidden from the guard and anyone else within earshot. Really good.

"So you shot out the tire from a mile away?"

"Thirteen hundred feet actually." She wasn't

bragging just talking while she started up the turbines.

"That is a hell of a shot. I have to thank you for saving my ass again."

"That's what I'm here for." Again not bragging.

"Ok if I sit up front?" Matt wondered.

"Yup, just close the hatch and we are outta here."

Matt slammed the door closed and took the co-pilots seat. He was feeling the stress of the last few days and his back was really killing him now that he thought about it.

They were barely in the air and he was asleep. He didn't even say one word to his pilot before nodding off.

~

When Matt woke it was dark. The cockpit was lit up like a Christmas tree all green and red with gauges and dials.

"Hey, sleepy head. Feel any better?" Matt had almost forgot that he was thirty thousand feet over the Atlantic in a private jet.

"Hey, yea, just a little groggy from lack of sleep and all the excitement I guess."

"You could probably use a cleanup." The captain offered.

"Smell a little do I?" Matt queried.

"Just a little." She laughingly replied. "There's a shower in the back head. Some soap and shampoo and a couple of clean towels too."

"All the modern conveniences."

"Pretty sure we liberated this from some drug lord or big-time gangster who wanted it to be just like home. That's why you had the luxury of a bed when the doctor was looking after you."

"Well, a great big thank you to whoever had the foresight," Matt said as he unbuckled and headed back to see if he could wash up at least.

The head was better than what he expected. The bulkhead had been modified to allow for an almost full height shower head. The space was big enough for him to actually move around in. Once in the water was hot and steady and felt great. Looked like there were some clean clothes that might just fit as well. They had thought of everything.

He had finished washing and was just rinsing his hair when he thought he heard the door to the bathroom open and close. Maybe he hadn't closed it tight when he came in, he thought.

He poked his head out from behind the tiny curtain just to make sure and was surprised to see the captain standing in the space.

"Hey." He said.

'Hey. She said back as she began to unbutton her blouse. "It's been a long day for me too. How about sharing the shower?"

"It's pretty tight in here," Matt replied.

"I think it's going to get a lot tighter." She laughed.

"Who's flying the plane?" Matt wondered.

"Otto." She said.

"Very funny. But should Otto be given so much authority at this altitude."

"Well, it wouldn't be much fun if there wasn't some small element of risk, would it?

"If I'm going to risk Otto at the helm I guess I can risk getting stuck in here with you, miss?"

"Marianna." She said as she slipped into the tiny shower stall.

The rest of the three thousand miles it would take to get to New York was spent chatting in the cockpit with a couple of intervals for testing the co-pilots chair to see if it fit two. Marianna explained to Matt that the jet had been outfitted with extra fuel tanks to give it greater range so they would have no trouble crossing the Atlantic. Because of the maximum range speed for a given total load with only the two of them on board and the fact that they were in no hurry so they could fly at a speed that was the most fuel efficient, the crossing would be lengthy but pretty easy.

Matt dozed on and off. They would be in New York ten days before the cargo ship USS Algon made port. Matt thought that he could use the break. He had not expected so much excitement in Africa. When they landed he would take a couple of days and heal up. His back felt like some of the stitches had popped while he was ducking and weaving on the dock in Douala. It wasn't the worst pain he had ever felt but bad enough.

Then he needed to research the Algon and find out where it would dock and when.

NEW YORK

Matt had properties in a number of cities around the world. Beijing, Leningrad, Toronto, Manilla, New York and many more. Small out of the way places. Not lavish but not uncomfortable, just inconspicuous hidey holes where he kept the cash and equipment he needed to do his job in any situation.

New York was a quiet little one bedroom apartment on Morton Street in Lower Manhattan. Quaint brownstones lined the sidewalks. The pub down the end of the row had been there for a hundred years as did a number of its patrons. It was the perfect place to recoup and plan to intercept the ivory stowaways where ever they made port.

After a perfect landing at LaGuardia's business center, the travel companions parted ways, Matt joking about getting together under less stressful circumstances and Marianna suggesting that that would likely be impossible. Not that they would never see one another again but that the situation would almost certainly be stressful.

His cab was waiting on the other side of the small customs building that serviced the business terminal. Matt was almost asleep by the time they reached his

171

apartment but he had the cabbie drop him at Rafele's, a little restaurant and bar at Morton and 7th Ave. He had no bags to carry and it was literally half a block to the brownstone second-floor apartment.

He just needed a cold beer and some good home cooked Italian pasta before he crashed. The last couple of days had been epic and he was still wound up tighter than a bull's ass in fly season. The unexpected sex with Marianna had only helped with some of the tension, he needed to go over where he had made mistakes and put Africa behind him before going to the apartment.

A cold beer turned into five. The pasta was what one would expect from a good Italian restaurant in New York City. The sauce was perfectly garliced and the pasta andante with just enough cilantro to open the nostrils. It was just what he needed. A big heavy meal before bed.

After paying the check Matt wandered down the street taking in the smells of New York in the late spring and reveling in the feeling of being back in America. He barely remembered climbing the stairs of the Brownstone or opening the windows to air the place out. He didn't even make the bed just curled up on the couch and was gone.

~

When Matt woke up it was dark outside. He dragged himself off the couch and climbed into bed.

It was noon the next day when he finally woke up. He had really needed the healing time. He could still feel the stitches in his back but they didn't hurt anymore and that was good.

First order of the day was to visit the market and get some supplies. There was nothing in the apartment. Matt hadn't been there for six months. After opening all the windows he got a clean pair of jeans out of the closet and a green t-shirt and headed down to the corner market. It was one of those little old traditional Italian places with the wicker buckets out front that presented all the good stuff, apples, oranges, melons and anything that gave off an aroma and was brightly colored. Sometimes the owner lost an apple or two to street kids but that was just all part of doing business in the neighborhood.

It was a grocery store more than anything else but the owner, Tony, kept a few steaks and some sliced meats, just enough to keep you going over a weekend if you ran out. He also stocked the other stuff you would need on the fly like toothbrushes, razors, soaps, beer, anything that people in the hood might run out of on any given day.

Matt picked up some things. A couple of steaks,

pasta noodles and the groceries he would need for a few days in the apartment. He also grabbed a six pack of beer. It was late spring in New York and that meant he would likely get a couple of humid days while he was here. Might as well mitigate the heat with a cold beverage.

With the bags of groceries tucked under each arm, Matt headed back to the apartment to start planning his reception for the stolen ivory.

~

Food put away and lunch finished Matt pulled a watertight, fireproof case out from under the bed and threw it up on the kitchen table. The apartment had a very open design. The kitchen and dining area were almost one and the same. They were separated by a very cool island that acted as a prep area when cooking and had room for four bar stools that gave more seating to the space. His kitchen slash dining room table sat six but was rectangular and fit the apartment like a glove. The rest of the space was taken up with the usual trappings of any New York apartment. Couch, love seat and chair surrounded a copper coffee table and all were strategically placed to maximize the centerpiece of the room, the fireplace. Built in the 1860's the brownstone boasted that every apartment had a fireplace. Matt's was very cool. The apartment was once the original kitchen area of the old home and was the central point for the family of the house at the time. Big enough to hold a full-on campfire, it still contained the metal pot rods anchored in the side walls that were originally used to hang cooking pots over the roaring blazes.

Matt kept the flu clean so on any given winter night he was able to start a fire that was Norman Rockwell in its brilliance.

Tonight was not one of those nights as Matt pulled his laptop, GPS, and his digital notepad out of the case he had so unceremoniously dumped on the table, He cracked one of his beers and settled in to try and track down the Algon's point port.

Since cargo ships didn't need to log a travel schedule like an airliner would issue a flight plan Matt would have to determine the Algon's bond port. That was the vessels initial customs entry to a country or first port of call. Matt hoped the Algon was headed for the US. He based his assumption on the fact that it was a US registered cargo ship. It could have just as easily headed south when it left port in Douala but he was betting that he would find it off the coast of Africa headed west. He was hoping to access the same satellite system that had monitored the explosion of the warehouse in Bertoua. First, he would have to locate the Algon then he would have to monitor its travel to make sure it was headed for America and to which port. He would set up a bi-daily satellite system to keep it under surveillance to find out where it was headed.

First things first, He had to find the ship. That would not be as easy as you would think. Even with sophisticated satellite systems at his disposal, there were hundreds of ships at any one time in any few thousand miles of the Atlantic. He would just guess at its speed and heading and start looking.

The call to TUSC was brief. Just long enough to request his access to the satellites. He was given some coordinates which he fed into a Skystar 2 PCI satellite receiver card he had purchased on eBay along with an open source DVB software app and a data analysis sniffing tool.

Using these tools, Matt was able to create an untraceable anonymous connection to the satellite and basically command it to look for whatever he programmed it to search.

Two days earlier while fleeing for his life, Matt had tried to scan the deck of the ship as he ran. He was looking for the gunman who had almost taken him out with the first couple of shots.

He had no luck in that pursuit but he did notice the

shipping containers that had been on deck.

Stacked to three high, he had retained a mental image of their approximate color array. Blue on gray beside umber. Set in a random but recognizable pattern. He could use this small bit of info along with the satellites ability to take images in stereo-optic pairs (that meant that more than one satellite could take side by side images at slightly different angles) then with digital technology they could string these images together to get a 3D view of the object under surveillance. Matt could literally look for the unique pattern of shipping containers and at the same time match them up with a side view of the ship giving him a satellite view of her name on the bulkhead.

He settled in and started to scan the ocean. He was approximating using an average speed for a ship of her size and the assumption that she would be taking the shortest route to America.

It was surprising how many ships were crossing the Atlantic at the same time. Matt knew that the airways over North America were literally jam-packed with aircraft but he had no idea there would be so many ships on their way from the African continent to the US. He also hadn't counted on them having similar cargo.

Even though he had a pretty clear visual of the

colored containers on the deck of the Algon, he had already fully vetted three likely vessels with no luck. Even with the satellite 3D imagery, it took him the better part of the night to find what he was looking for.

It was well after midnight when Matt looked up from his computer screen and noticed the time and the six empty beer cans. His neck was cramped from craning over the laptop and when he stood up he could feel the beers he hadn't even remembered drinking.

He made his way to the bedroom swaying just a little, on the computer screen, left open on the kitchen table, the Algon stood out on a sea of dark foreboding water it's multicolored cargo bins stacked on deck and the 3D image of her name standing out against a sea-hardened and rusting hull.

The days ahead would tell him more of her course and destination.

MASTER

It took a full two years for Matt to absorb everything Master Machida could give. The old master himself was astounded at the rapidity of the young man's understanding not just of the Kata's but of the essence, structure and belief system of the art. Matt had been only too happy to study everything the Master had given him.

Once Master Machida understood the innate ability that the student had he had bypassed many traditional plateaus of the teaching process and given him trials that men who had studied all their lives could not understand let alone perfect.

Matt had come to these tests like a child to a coloring book. Often painting the traditional moves of the ancient Kata's with different colors and finding new ways to improve on the angle of a kick or the pressure of a blow.

Matt had not come through the year without trial. The other students were not so eager to just let him be the one. They didn't resent his ability, they just wanted him to know that they were no less passionate. Their passion kept Matt on his toes. If he flinched even for a second any one of them would not hesitate to use the opportunity to leave a bruise on his body.

That was fine with Matt. He had never taken any of his skill for granted. There was one test that the Master put them all too. One that Matt swore the old man enjoyed.

It was a lesson in pain.

He would make the students sit in the lotus position remaining completely motionless for an hour. Eventually, their legs hurt so much every one of them wanted to scream but no one wanted to show any sign of weakness.

As they all sat in the courtyard the old man would walk among them with a four-foot-long wooden paddle. As he walked through the group a student would raise his hands in front of him, palms together in prayer position. He would then lean forward to expose his back. The old man standing in front would bow to the student and then smack him twice on each shoulder. The student would then return to sitting in the lotus position without showing any signs of the obvious pain he was in.

The first time Matt experienced the shoulder smacks he could not believe the pain. It sounded like a gunshot each time the paddle landed. He thought he was going to puke right there in the middle of the group. It was all he could do to sit still and act like he felt nothing.

Matt eventually steeled his mind to the agony of these blows but he never let on one way or the other but accepted the torture as part of the training.

It was on the last night of Matt's stay in Okinawa that he was summoned to dinner before everyone else. He arrived to see the Master sitting at the short-legged table that was the evening dining table, head bent contemplating a cup of tea.

"You asked to see me," Matt spoke in a quiet tone so as not to startle the old man.

"There is no need to whisper." The Master replied. "I am quite capable of hearing you."

"I was only trying not to disturb your contemplation," Matt explained.

"There is no need to explain. I know what your intent was. Please sit. I want to talk to you before the rest arrive for dinner."

Matt sat, cross-legged on the other side of the chabudai. He could see no turmoil in the older man's movements or demeanor so he wondered if this was just his way of saying goodbye.

"This year you have brought great honor to my humble Dojo. In all my years as an instructor, I have never seen anyone like you. You have a gift, more than a gift. It is something that legends are made of and many would kill to possess."

Matt, to say the least, was stunned. He had envisioned a way to go and stop by any time you're in town kinda chat.

In the last two years, Matt had added muscle and some mass to his six foot two frame. He had gone from a skilled student of the art to a lethal one man fighting machine. His stamina was next to none and he was able to out-think anyone in a confrontational or insurgent situation. He had exhausted the old master's teachings and was ready for a new challenge.

"You are no longer the student but the teacher and I must bow to your special understanding of the art."

And with that, the old man stood and bowed deeply to the younger man at the table.

When he had sat down again, Master Matchida's demeanor changed and Matt was once again a guest in the old man's home. Getting ready for the evening meal.

"Please, before the others arrive, tell me what it is you believe you will do in life."

This was a question that Matt had begun to contemplate the last six months of his training. Under the strict rules of the art and the house he lived in, Matt had come to realize that his ability was something more than average. He also realized that he had an opportunity to do something with it. He knew now that he could become more than just a Karate teacher back in Chicago.

Ethan was coming to Japan tomorrow to pick him up and see his old Master one more time. He had planned on getting some advice from him on the trip back to Chicago. One thing for sure, he was not going to be able to go back to working for the Parks and Recreation Department of Chicago when he got home.

~

"I have been thinking of that for some time now Master," Matt replied. "I have some ideas but I want to run them by Ethan on the way back to the States and get his opinion first."

"You have a great opportunity to do good with your gift. I hope you find a way to use it to better the world we live in."

The Master bowed again this time without getting up. Matt bowed back just in time for the rest of the students living at the Dojo to come boisterously into the room for dinner.

~

The next morning seemed odd and sad in a way. It was the first time in two years that Matt hadn't gotten up to the first rays of the morning sun, put on his gi and headed for the central court to start his training for the day. He would normally be anxious to get going. For the last six months every day the Master had tried to stump him with more and more difficult training scenarios and tests. Each time after giving him some new Kata to train for only a day or two and then springing some inventive way of testing the new moves or skill.

To this point, Matt had ingested the technique and spit it back out in test after test. Never once failing to accomplish what he had been tasked to do.

The other students never once complained that he was getting special treatment. Matt treated them as if they were brothers and he secretly thought that they didn't really want any part of the training he was personally going through, not once had he told them what his special training was like. He could see that they were just as happy to keep up their studies the way they were.

This had been the time when Matt realized that he

was different. That he had a skill that others did not. It was up to him to try and define how he would use it. What was it he felt about it? Could Ethan help him channel his thoughts and new found ability so that he would be a force in the world?

Matt still remembered being robbed his first night in Chicago. That feeling had stuck with him. In someone else, it may have led to a life of bitterness and anger toward those that took advantage of the weak and unwary but in Matt, it just reaffirmed his need to do something to protect those that could not protect themselves. He could not have known then that in the next two years he would find that calling back in the USA.

~

Ethan arrived just before the classes scheduled midday break and after having lunch with Master Machida and the rest of the students Matt and Ethan loaded his gear, which was still pretty sparse, into the back of the Toyota Rav4 and headed to the other side of the island where Ethan had rented a couple of hotel rooms in the city of Naha. They were going to spend a few days celebrating Matt's end of training and have a little fun in the city.

THE ALGON

The Algon was definitely heading for the Northern United States. Matt had been keeping a watchful eye on the vessel since his marathon satellite search eight days earlier. If it stayed on course it looked like he would be within jumping distance of it when it made port. If he really got lucky, given its current trajectory, it might even dock somewhere in the New York Harbor system.

That remained to be seen. It wouldn't make land for another twenty-four hours at its present speed so Matt was just killing time until it did.

He had spent a few solitary hours cleaning some of his handguns and the one larger weapon he kept in the New York apartment but he could feel the anxiety of his encounter with the soon to dock freighter starting to get the better of him. Best to get out of the house and get some fresh air and sunshine. He had found himself thinking of Marianna and wondered if he would be lucky enough to see her again before this particular mission was over. Now that his back had healed and he had a number of nights of solid sleep under his belt he was chapping at the bit to get back to tracking the load of ivory he had followed across Africa and now across the Atlantic Ocean.

He knew he couldn't be distracted by Marianna but it was a nice thought on a sunny May afternoon as he walked the dock side of Battery Park and looked up at the new construction that rose like a Phoenix from the solemn holes at ground zero. The sight of the memorials and the ongoing construction re-affirmed his commitment to track terrorism in any form. As long as their activity brought harm to the shores of the United States of America and put innocent people in harm's way, he would track down the smugglers, the gun runners, the recruiters, those that would hide behind the security of walled states and firewalled computer screens and bring down their money-making enterprises, disrupt their avenues for laundering the ill-gotten millions and if, in the process, a few bad people did not survive so be it.

The crazy thing was chasing down the ivory poachers was becoming more of a quest than just doing his job. He really felt like he was doing something to stay the reckless slaughter of an endangered species.

He realized that putting an end to this one underground chain would only put a small dint in the poaching of African elephants and other endangered animals but if he could follow the connection started with the murder of the Matriarch, so many days ago, to its end he would be able to put

187

a much bigger dent in the workings of one of a hundred terror cells that currently used the illegal sale of the ivory to fund their crazed agendas.

He would have to wait and see. He would know better by the end of the day. The Algon would have had time to show her stripes. At least she would be close enough to the continent so he could make a good guess as to her destination.

Once the port was more defined he would confirm with TUSC and get the exact port of call and the container terminal coordinates. Nothing to do but wait.

Back at the brownstone, Matt took the few hours before he checked on the Algon to grab a nap. If Africa was an indicator, it might be a while before he got to sleep again so a little in the bank never hurt. He lay down and was immediately asleep, his laptop open and waiting for the sun to sink behind the cityscape of New York to light the room with its luminescent glow. It was also rigged with a pretty loud alarm that woke Matt out of a deep black hole three hours later. It had been set to let Matt know when the Algon had passed a certain point enroute. Its wailing complaint was the negotiation of that milestone.

Matt bolted out of bed drawn to the light of the computer screen like a moth to the back door light.

The Algon was mid-screen and headed right for New York Harbor.

It couldn't have worked out better. Now he would call TUSC and get them to hack the ship's computer to find out its exact port of call. Matt would be waiting and this time he was on home turf. He wouldn't have to rely on rundown SUVs and unfamiliar streets. They were in his ballpark now. Shit was going to hit the fan.

SHIPMATES

Matt's phone call rendered all the information he needed. The ship was docking in Port Newark in the Elizabeth Channel. Hell, he knew that area well. There were all kinds of rundown storage areas just south of the channel and the 95. They were easily accessible from the Newark Liberty International Airport so he had great access to the pier from any number of vantage points. Better yet he could just drive right up to it from the access road off of the 95 and Tyler Street and park right in the port authority parking lot. If he just dressed in jeans and a worn jacket, he would look like every other dock worker. No one would give him a second look.

~

One thing Matt was sure of. The ivory that he had tailed from out on the Savanah to the port here in New York would not be lonely. There would be more than those two tusks. These guys wouldn't risk jail for a paltry three or four hundred thousand. The smugglers would have enough ivory hidden on board to net in the millions once auctioned off on the black market. Matt had no doubt that he would recognize it when they tried to get it ashore.

Ivory was never stored in the big freight containers.

Too much could go wrong. All the containers pretty much looked the same. It wouldn't be the first time a would-be smuggler screwed up because he lost a shipping container on a doc where there were thousands of others that looked exactly alike. Even if they kept track of their prize there was too much risk of it being spot checked by the port authority before it got off the dock. No, it would come off the ship in the middle of unloading the larger cargo. That way it would be less conspicuous and it would be in a small enough container, probably wooden crates or one large wooden crate, so it could be easily transported by a pickup or a cargo van.

Even a decent sized shipment would be worth millions and Matt was following those millions right to the source hopefully breaking up the chain of command in the process.

~

Morning came early with the usual sounds and smells of another bustling New York day getting its feet wet.

Matt dragged his 1975 Norton Commando out from under the tarp in the back of the brownstone. It had been hiding there since he had left for Africa.

Matt loved all things two-wheeled and he had a few.

The Norton was just one of a number of classic motorcycles that he had purchased over the years. Some he bought fully restored others he had put some elbow grease and a few hundred hours into getting road worthy.

His tastes weren't limited to great old bikes he had a number of scooters and a few pedal bikes that ranged from a competitive carbon fiber mountain bike to a sleek Kevlar time trial machine specifically designed for triathlon.

Today it was the Norton Commando. It was perfect for the task at hand. He would need reliable, fast transportation in case he had to follow his prize. Something that could go just about anywhere. It was easier to hide than a full sized car or truck and made the perfect vehicle for slipping through traffic if need be.

He had always maintained the bike even if he wasn't using it and it started right up. The sound of the 750cc engine reverberated through the tiny backyards of the block and the smooth idling belayed its immense torque off the line. Matt kicked the shift into first and hit the streets headed for the New Jersey Turnpike and the port of Newark. Once he was across the bridge it would be a short cruise to the port authority and the Elizabeth Channel docks.

Matt had the mooring schedule for the Algon and

its arrival time. He knew exactly where he had to be and at what time. He left some minutes in for traffic and hit the New Jersey Turnpike just as the sun came up over the lower bay. The smells of the harbor wafted up over the bridge deck as he crossed into New Jersey. The transit water and dead fish fragrance was only canceled out by the ever-present aura of creosote that permeated every dockside in every town or city that made its living from the sea worldwide. He loved it. It was harsh and refreshing at the same time.

He turned left onto Corban Street off the bridge and was in the port authority in two minutes. He took Marsh to Export St. and was parking his bike in the Eastern Metal Recycling parking lot three minutes after that.

The parking lot was perfect. No one was going to question the bike in this place. People came and went all day long here. Other than the fact that it was a nice looking old Norton it would just be another bike.

It was just over two hundred meters from the parking lot to where the Algon was moored. If he had to Matt could make that distance in just over thirty seconds. Far enough away for the bike to be inconspicuous to those on deck and close enough for him to get to fast.

Matt walked up Clipper Street between the two huge warehouses, not in a hurry just another employee going about his day. He nodded to a person leaning against an open door as he made his way out across Starboard Street and into the container field that led to where the Algon was birthed and waiting to be offloaded.

As Matt came to the end of the long line of containers, he stopped and kept hidden behind a large orange railway car left to wait for its transport.

The gantry cranes looked like they were just getting started on the Algon and Matt had a perfect line of sight to the entire length of the ship. If the ivory was coming off here, he wouldn't miss it.

The Algon was an average container vessel but it still could potentially hold about thirty-five hundred containers. That would make for a long day if the bad guys waited for most of them to be off before moving the smuggled ivory. Matt was quite sure they wouldn't wait that long.

He was right but it was still an hour later when he caught the illegal cargo coming off the ship. He had to hand it to them. They were smart. He was also wrong in his assumption that they wouldn't offload the illegal booty in a standard container. The crate he had seen going on the ship in Douala was long gone. In its place was what to the layman's eye look like just another container being lifted to the dock. The difference was this one was about eight feet longer than the previous two hundred that had already been placed dockside. The extra eight feet had been strategically shaped to match a typical railway box and painted with the same flat orange to match. It was the perfect ruse.

Matt followed its lazy arc as the crane swung out over the yard and deposited its oversized load. Now another waiting game began. It could be days before the container was picked up.

Matt thought not. The traffickers would want to get it off the lot in a hurry. They would have already made all the arrangements for the Ocean Bill of Lading and more than likely bribed someone to take control of the shipment and customs clearing. He would wait. This time back to the front of the line of containers to see what big rig grabbed the oversize package and then while the truck negotiated its way out of the big box labyrinth he would sprint back to his bike and be waiting in the parking lot for it to pass. He would also leave a little something for the port authority to suggest that they should take a closer look at the cargo manifest of the Algon. There was a good chance that the ship would have been carrying more than one illegal crate at a time.

SUNDAY DRIVE

He didn't have to wait long. The cargo container with the extended rear end had only been on the ground minutes before a big shiny blue American built Peterbilt semi-trailer backed up beside the container that Matt was watching. A large man in blue jeans and a tee shirt swung his overfed belly down from the cab and waited while the on-ship crane took time out from its focused effort to get the remaining containers off the ship to quickly pick the illegal container off the dock and place it lightly on the waiting rig.

The driver quickly turned the pin locks and secured the cargo. His belly clearly getting in the way as he took two attempts to get back into the idling rig and under the steering wheel.

The truck rumbled right past where Matt was standing but the driver didn't take his eyes off the prize. He pushed right down Starboard Street, making his way between the rows of boxcar containers and turned left onto Export Street on his way to Corbin and from their I95 and away.

Matt waited for the driver to turn left at the end of the holding area and then sprinted back to the

197

Norton its engines coming to life with one kick of the starter.

He waited patiently for the truck to reappear as it came out around the end of the warehouses and headed for the highway. When the truck turned onto Corbin making its way to the off-ramp at the I95 he popped the clutch and followed at a distance to see what direction the driver would take. North toward Boston or south toward Washing DC.

At this point, there was little traffic between Matt and the exiting semi but the driver took a right before Port Street which definitely meant he was headed for the highway. Matt would not know which direction he would go until they connected with the 78 and took one of the many options at the cloverleaf at the 95.

It took ten minutes for the semi to get to the cloverleaf. Matt had waited on the edge of the Port Authority Administration building. From his vantage point, he had a clear view of the highway and the overpass where the rig would have to pass on its way north or south.

Sun glinted like a laser ray off the polished chrome grill on the Peterbilt as it turned north. If he stayed on this route the rig would pass thousands of possible drop points. Matt would not be able to keep as low a profile as he had hoped. He had hoped that he would be able to follow the truck from afar giving it a wide berth and being as inconspicuous as possible. Now he would have to stay closer to the rig just in case it made a quick exit along the way.

Matt gunned the engine and raced after the retreating truck. He didn't think that it would make any quick turns at this point but you never knew and he couldn't take any chance of losing the ivory he had been following for so long.

Matt followed his prize back along the 95, over the George Washington Bridge and back into New York. Tremont, West Farms and Van Nest flew by in minutes. As the highway turned North, Bay Chester and Eastchester pointed the way to New Rochell. Now the countryside turned to suburbia with tree-lined communities and golf courses. By the time they were passing Riverside Matt had a gut feeling that the rig was headed for Boston or at least one of the many secluded smaller harbors that lined the seaside on the way to that great city.

He also had been trying to keep a constant distance behind the semi but he was becoming concerned. Not because he thought he would be detected. He was too far back for that but because there were a couple of other vehicles that were keeping a pretty constant distance behind the Peterbilt too. A Ford

Escape and a little Honda Civic had been trading places for over forty-five minutes. Usually, that wouldn't have been unusual because by this point Matt would have passed the semi up the road and would have been long on his way to where ever he was going. But since the two vehicles had gone by him and then let him go by them a number of times meant they were either following the truck as well or they were making sure no one else was following the rig.

Matt would have to back off or go around and wait up the road for the semi-trailer to go buy. He needed to ditch the bike and find another way to keep up.

By the time the transport made Bridgeport, Matt was certain that the two vehicles he had noticed following the truck were probably doing just that. They had passed and repassed him a couple of more times in the last few miles and while neither one had looked over nor made any moves that would have said "we see you," He was pretty sure that they were hired guns. Just like at the port in Africa, there had been a second team in place in case anyone got too close to the smugglers or their operation.

Matt decided that it would be prudent to arrange to pick up another mode of transport and soon.

The next time both of the suspect cars were ahead of him on the road, Matt pulled a cell phone from his saddlebag and dialed the operator. When they answered Matt asked to be put through to any car rental place in New Haven. His call was immediately picked up by a friendly female voice that asked how she could be of service.

Matt explained that he was about fifteen miles away and was having trouble with his bike. He was in a hurry to get to a meeting in Bangor Maine and needed a good reliable car by the time he got to town.

"What exactly are you looking for sir?" the girl asked. "We've had a run on compacts and SUVs in the last couple of days so we are a bit down on stock."

"Actually, I would like something a bit sporty if you have. Maybe a Mustang or a Camaro?"

"I can tell you we have both of those vehicles on the lot sir as I am looking at them out front of the showroom window right now."

"Can you please get the paperwork ready to a point on any one of those two cars and I will have my credit card ready for you when I get there likely in about ten minutes or less."

"I should be able to get that done sir. There will be

a walk around inspection before you can leave the lot. I hope you have time for that?"

"Absolutely," Matt replied. "I might even be there a bit faster. Can you text me your coordinates to the number you see on your phone?"

"On their way." The girl replied.

With that, Matt tucked the phone into his bomber jacket pocket and cranked the throttle.

He didn't look around as he flew past the two escort vehicles and half a minute later the Peterbilt. He just kept the hammer down until he got to the outskirts of New Haven. Then he pulled off the side of the road and copied the rental office address into his Google Map app on the phone.

He was in luck. The address was only a few blocks away. The Google lady told him he would reach his destination in seven minutes. That was good because he was sure that he would have some catching up to do once he got through the process of renting the car and getting back on the road.

~

The girl at the rental office was as good as her word. She didn't waste time explaining the ins and outs of the contract she just took Matt's information and credit card, walked him around the new Camaro

SC600.

It was perfect. Matt made an inquiry about leaving his bike until he could get someone to come and get it and the girl assured him that they would take it into the shop until he returned.

With that Matt was behind the wheel and headed back out to chase down the rig.

The Camaro had that new car smell and right away he could feel the power of the four hundred and fifty-five horsepower engine under the hood.

He hit the 95 flying. He didn't think the tusks would take any side trips around here but better safe than sorry.

The Camaro hit a hundred in seconds and it wasn't long before Matt picked up the familiar profile of the little Honda Civic. The little car stood out with its gaudy fishtail spoiler hanging on for dear life on the trunk but Matt thought it was more functional than not. If his assumption was correct and the Civic was, in fact, an escort vehicle then the spoiler would come in handy on any possible high-speed chase or run.

Matt decided to stay well back. As long as he could see one or the other of the two cars up ahead he could be assured that the rig was

203

just up ahead as well.

~

Matt didn't listen to the radio. He found that music could distract and right now he needed his wits about him. The job at hand wasn't so tough. Really, driving along an open highway following a big truck and a couple of support cars was pretty easy. The hard part was doing so without making the subject vehicles aware of what he was doing. Besides, there were a thousand places the rig could turn of this highway and if it did and what he had assumed were support vehicles kept going he could just as easily keep going along with them and he would lose his target.

Matt had to be vigilant. He watched out his side mirror as a small gray Toyota Sienna pulled alongside him. He glanced over to see who was behind the wheel as he was still just south of a hundred miles an hour and for someone to pass they would have to be over that.

He was shocked to see a rather elderly Asian woman. What surprised him more was when she boldly turned to face him before hitting the brakes just enough so she could let him drift by and then pulled to the right lightly tapping the corner of his rear bumper to send the Camaro into a very dangerous sideways skid.

Matt had only enough time to think, hey that was a pro move before the car started to correct itself and jagged back to the left as the tires caught the pavement. If he didn't act quickly, he would end up in the ditch or event worse upside down and slammed into any number of obstacles along the roadside.

The elderly Asian woman had used the PIT maneuver (Precision Immobilization Technique) on him. A pursuit tactic that causes the object car to abruptly turn sideways, causing the driver to either lose control or to slam on the brakes and stop.

Fortunately for Matt, the old lady had waited until they had passed over the bridge that spanned the Connecticut River if he had of lost control there it would have been the drink or into an oncoming car.

Here they were well beyond the water and into some of the dense woodlands that bordered the 95 or as it was called here the Connecticut Turnpike.

There could only be one reason for the attack to come in this sparsely inhabited eight-mile stretch of highway. They were on to him and they wanted to know who he was and why he would be following a cargo truck up the coast of the USA.

As the Camaro came to its zenith going left, Matt

waited for the inertia to drive the frame back the way it had come. The whiplash caused by the tires grabbing the road as the car slid left almost took Matt's hands off the wheel. He just grabbed it back in time to hit the brakes full on as the swaying car hit its neutral point. That just happened to be in the middle of the highway and caught his pursuer completely by surprise. As the Toyota blew past Matt was already on the gas and the extra horsepower under the hood of the rental put him within an inch of the would-be assailant's bumper still traveling at about one hundred miles an hour. It was almost too easy to tap the bumper of the Sienna and send it into the ditch digging up clumps of dirt and grass as it went and eventually catching both the right tires and slamming over on its side.

Matt screamed to a sliding stop, not twenty feet from where the van had gone down into the ditch and jumped out. He was around the side of the van in seconds and he could see that the driver was out cold. It had come to rest precariously teetering on its side. Not wanting to lose the convoy while he dealt with this unexpected event, Matt just used his own body weight to push the van onto its hood exposing both windows at ground level.

The woman basically fell out the window as the van went over. Her silenced Beretta 93R came with her. Matt was amazed. It was obvious that the woman was no spring chicken and had to be at least in her late sixties. What the hell was she doing running down someone in broad daylight in the middle of Massachusetts?

He didn't have time to ponder the craziness of it. He had to get back on the road. Matt picked up the weapon and headed back to the car but not before applying a little trick he had learned in Japan.

~

Matt's time in Japan wasn't all just kicking and punching. There were many days spent in the pursuit of the finer sciences of the art. They could spend a whole day often eight or ten hours sitting in one position, no matter if it was the heat of the day or a raging downpour. Sometimes they would spend hours perfecting one attack and one defense to the point where both the attacker and the defender would have no feeling in their arms or legs. Even at that, if the master felt their technique lacked finesse the whole routine would be re-performed the next day until he decided they had got it right.

One of Matt's favorite disciplines was pressure points or meridian points. Used in a gentler arena, it was called Acupressure and could release tense muscle and nerves to relieve everything from back pain to headache.

In Karate, the use of meridian points to immobilize or incapacitate an assailant had been around forever.

Originally brought to light by Minamoto Yoshimitsu who lived from 1045 to 1127. He was credited with bringing the art of meridian points into martial arts fighting. The skill also included the controversial Death Touch known in Japanese as kyusho jitsu. This touch method if performed correctly could, in fact, kill someone.

Matt loved the intricacies of the art. Like much of his other intuitive ways this particular skill came to him like flies to honey. He could almost see his subject's chi pulsing in their body and he could pinpoint the nerves with astonishing accuracy. He would even pay his fellow trainees to let him practice the pressure points on them. It didn't take him long to run out of volunteers pay or no pay but by then he had developed a perfect pressure point attack that would always leave his opponent unconscious. He also knew that if he used just the right amount of pressure that person would not wake up from their unexpected nap.

~

Matt knelt quickly beside the fallen woman and gently tapped a small nerve ending and a tiny blood vessel just behind her ear. The simultaneous pressure at these cross points would keep her asleep for a long time. Even if EMT's tried to rouse her they would assume trauma-induced coma.

With that, he grabbed the Berretta and ran back to the highway where a couple of good Samaritans were exiting their cars above the ditch. He jumped back into the rental, spraying grass and gravel as he hit the highway and quickly got the Camaro back up to speed.

He had to be cautious now. The other safety cars would not know that he had evaded the trap they had set with the Asian lady. But he couldn't pass them now either.

Matt knew sometimes that the best defense was offense. As he made up ground on the ivory convoy he decided that if either of the other two vehicles were far enough apart for him to take one out he would do it. It wouldn't be so uncommon for a hit and run to leave a vehicle in the ditch and take off down the road. Traffic was light and if there happened to be other traffic involved they would be more interested in the car that was in trouble than the one that was speeding away.

What happened next couldn't have been more perfect. As he raced along highway 95 in hot pursuit of the rig and its accompanying entourage, a late model Mustang passed Matt in a hurry. Matt was doing well over a hundred so the Mustang was really laying on the gas.

Matt wasted no time getting in behind the speeding Mustang. He would ride this speed junkie's tail right up to the next trailing point man.

As they were now doing in excess of one hundred and thirty miles an hour it didn't take long for Matt to spot the first follow car up ahead. The driver of the Mustang had not slowed down or changed lanes in the few minutes it had taken to catch the traffic. Matt was certain the follow car would have noticed the high rate of speed the two cars were traveling but he hoped that because there were two of them, it would give him a few seconds of surprise. That along with the rate of speed they would be on the car in moments.

It was the shitty little Honda Civic with the gaudy spoiler. Matt was pretty sure the poor bugger never knew what hit him.

The two speeding sports cars caught the Honda so fast he didn't really have time to react. Sitting in the Mustangs slipstream, Matt marveled at how the car handled at speed. It was like sitting in a flying easy chair watching the big white oak trees that lined both sides of the highway fly by. The second the Mustang came alongside the Civic, Matt just eased out from behind the Mustang and tapped the left corner of the

Hondas rear bumper. Matt's speed kept him straight on the highway not even slowing as the little Japanese Honda went ass over tea kettle into the woods.

Matt watched as the car flipped right into the underbrush. There would be no warning call ahead from that lookout today.

If Matt had wondered whether there would be collateral damage from his taking out of the sentry he needn't have bothered. There was no one within half a mile of them and the Mustang, which was well on its way to trying to break the I95 speed record.

Matt let it go. He kept his foot on the gas because there was still no clear line of sight to the last follow car or the rig.

Another fifteen minutes, Matt caught the Peterbilt half way up a clover leaf-headed east toward the ocean with his little buddy in tow. This part of Maine was heavily wooded and Matt thought he had been extremely lucky to catch them before they had disappeared down this side road.

Matt couldn't know if the remaining escort car had been informed of his continued pursuit. He would have to follow at a distance that made the truck and its tag along feel safe until he could come up with a plan of attack.

The Peterbilt and the chase car had turned off at highway ninety-five and High Street, which led to the sleepy little town of Clinton Connecticut.

Clinton was as peaceful a town as you could imagine with about sixteen thousand residences. People went about their day never once imagining that there could be anything as dramatic as international smuggling and intrigue going on in their little village. In fact, the worst thing that had happened in Clinton since it was founded in sixteen sixty-three was on one bright sunny Easter Sunday, Jimmy Markham farted out loud in the middle of Reverend Martins sermon on the return of Christ.

Matt pulled off the road and into a parking spot at the Shell station that welcomed those who came that way to Clinton. He called up Google maps on his cell phone and typed in his location. The satellite feature on his Samsung Galaxy gave him a perfect view of the terrain and the layout of the little village. Matt traced High Street as it wandered toward the sound, twisting and turning, it sometimes changed its name until it finally came to an end in what Google said was Clinton harbor. It was the perfect place. From there, anyone with a boat had clear access to Long Island Sound and from there the ocean and the world.

One other thing Matt noticed was at the end of the

meandering street was a well-kept marina and at the very end of that marina was a building that sat right on the water's edge with perfect access for a big truck to back right up. Matt thought it would be really shitty luck if he made his way down to that point and he didn't see a big bright red Peterbilt semi-trailer backed up against it

He pocketed the phone and pulled the Camaro on to High Street. It was only a few minutes and he was at the marina.

The Harbor Side Marine and Repair was the hub of the community. There were plenty of cars parked in front and some of the locals were inside shooting the shit with the owner and picking up a few boating supplies. The Marine shop had been here since nineteen twenty-five so if you wanted to get your boat fixed or you needed to find out what happened at last week's council meeting, you headed there to get both.

The rest of the building was completely surrounded by boats. Some in for repair others brand new and waiting to be sold. Across the street was a vacant lot. It was fenced but there were large gaps in it so it could be used for overflow parking when things got busy on the weekends.

It was the perfect place for Matt to recon the docks

213

without being noticed. The dock he was interested in was on the north side of the Harbor Side Marine building and there were enough boats and other outbuildings in between to keep him well hidden as he made his way in that direction.

There was no fencing around any of the docks or warehouses. Even the Marine building and its lot full of boats had no security fence. Matt thought they must be a pretty trusting community or they had some really good video surveillance.

As he walked along the dock side of the inner quay he acted like he was interested in the watercraft lined up there. He only had to get beyond the first two bigger yachts to see a big red truck parked on the north side of the marina, backed up against the building he had targeted with the Google satellite maps. He could also see that the extension that he had spotted back in the shipyard had been removed. They had wasted no time in removing the false back containing the ivory from the rear of the Peterbilt. Obviously, they had broken it down and taken the contents inside.

He had an idea. From where he stood he could see a dinner partly hidden by the big truck. If he could get to the back door of the diner without causing any suspicion he could get around to the other side of the building from the dockside.

Matt walked casually out from the Marine yard and headed down to the diner. Shanks was written on a big sign out front and an open old wooden hulled sailboat, sans its mast and boom, parked by the front door acted as a takeout bar and cocktail lounge. The couple at the bar didn't look up as Matt went inside.

It was dark. The usual lantern lit seaside staging kept its place alongside the heavy odor of deep-fried fish. A middle-aged, aproned woman approached Matt from the confines of the kitchen.

"Just drinking or are you going to eat?" she asked.

"Both." Matt replied, "But I need to wash up first."

"Right around the back there." The woman pointed into the depths of an even darker hallway leading out the back of the restaurant.

"What do ya want to drink?" She hollered after him.

"Draft." Matt shot back.

Matt completely bypassed the men's and headed right into the women's washroom. No need to worry about occupancy, it was obvious there was no one else in the place and the women's was further back in the building than the men's.

215

Inside it was just as he had suspected. Buildings of this era relied on pretty big windows to keep the place cool even with central air in the summer windows were opened to air the places and let the sounds and the smells of the restaurant out.

This bathroom had a window large enough for Matt to easily escape and like the security that had been nonexistent at the Marine the women's bathroom at Shanks was no different. Matt just flipped the lock and crawled out right onto the dock behind his target.

It was only feet and Matt scrambled up to the building that looked like it too might have been a restaurant at one time and now abandoned or at least closed until further notice. It had probably been for rent and the smugglers saw the perfect opportunity to split up the ivory with access to the water for faster and less noticeable departure.

He had no idea of how many might be in the building. Judging by the number of cars and trucks around there could be as many as twenty or thirty. He didn't think so but he had to get a look inside to see what he was dealing with.

As he made his way to the other side of the landing he could hear voices through an open window. It sounded like negotiations. Matt knew he was onto an auction. This was good. An auction meant that there would be some high rollers here to bid on certain quantities and if he was really lucky he could shut down this pipeline to the ivory market and put a few shitty traffickers away. Hopefully one of them would want to talk about where the ivory would go next so he could follow that lead if need be but this would be the end of the line for the big money. After this, the ivory would be sectioned off and then carved up into trinkets and souvenirs to be sold overseas and in unscrupulous shops in America.

Matt had the Beretta and he unclipped the magazine to check on the rounds. It was full. He clipped it back in taking the gun off safety. He didn't want to waste any time with that if he didn't have too.

The voices from the window above were becoming more animated. One was definitely Chinese his heavy accent giving away his Cantonese heritage but there was more than one Asian in the room. The one who spoke in English occasionally spoke to someone else in his native tongue. That could only mean that there were at least two Chinese and an American who was obviously the contractor and financier for the ivory runners.

~

Matt had made it a point to learn both Japanese and Chinese while he was in Japan. He enjoyed the singsong quality of both these Asian dialects but preferred the more somber but essentially more meaningful language of Japan. He also hated that he couldn't understand what his fellow students were talking about and took great pains to hide the fact that eventually he not only could understand what they were saying but could hurl insults with more ardor than any old man from their fishing villages.

One night while sitting around the communal table a couple of the Japanese students had been discussing the fact that Matt must be getting secret coaching from the master. How else could he be so far ahead of everyone else and understand the nuances of the art like he had practiced for a hundred years? They kept referring him to him as "kusottare" which in English literally meant "shit drip"

Matt had listened silently with his usual pretense of not understanding what they were discussing but when they used the slang to describe him loud enough for the others to hear he quietly explained to them in perfect Japanese that he could help them "kuso kurae!" or in English "eat shit", if they liked.

The looks on their faces would have made almost anyone burst out laughing but Matt just stared them down to make sure they understood his meaning.

After that, the rest of the group became a little

friendlier toward him. It turned out the two troublemakers were just that and Matt calling them out had been a great relief for the rest of the students.

~

Matt snapped out of his revelry. This was no time for reminiscing. He had come a long way. Even still it felt like only a few days had gone by since he picked up the trail of the poachers in Africa and followed them all the way to this community dock in Connecticut.

He closed his eyes and breathed the salt air wafting in from the sound. It cleared his head as he lowered his heart rate and formulated a plan.

~

As Matt used the sound of the waves breaking against the pylons that held the docks in place to focus his mind he also calmed himself with a version of stomach breathing that he had learned from some cyclist friends of his in New York. It was a basic breathing technique that only required that you exhale all the breath from your lungs before inhaling your next. It was a simple but effective method of taking control of your respiratory system.

While he brought his body to center Matt was also planning a way into the building. The decision was helped along from an unexpected source.

Matt's hands were placed flat on the wooden planking that made up the entire expanse of the wharf. Even through the dense logs, he had felt the unmistakable vibration of someone walking on the dock on the front side of the building. He could tell by the slight differences in each vibration that whoever was out for a stroll was coming his way. Matt knew that it would only be someone assigned to guard the perimeter of the building to keep other users of the dock area at bay while the meeting went on inside.

Matt quickly calculated the seconds before the person generating the vibrations would round the corner and find him. He also determined the time it would take for him to reach that same corner from where he was hunkered down under the open window.

He was up and running in an instant. He had learned many things while he was in Japan and one of them that always in handy was the ability to run at top speed without making a sound. It was achieved by using a technique developed by race walkers and refined by hours of practice. While one foot is always on the ground the opposite foot lands heal first and roll through the motion instead of pushing off and becoming airborne. The method results in a very fast pace while almost completely silent.

Matt now used the method to fly at the corner of the building. His momentum got him there just in time to see a heavy fisted arm come into view holding a very slick Ruger LC9.

Matt knew that this was, in fact, a guard posted with only one purpose to keep the place free of onlookers and trouble.

After his encounter with the Asian woman who had tried to run him off the road and due to the fact that she had been carrying a very nasty little gun, he was taking no prisoners.

As the arm came fully around the edge of the building, Matt grabbed the wrist and using all his strength, he broke the ulna immobilizing the weapon while pulling the surprised assailant forward into a fatal punch to the throat.

The guy didn't make a sound and as he started to go down Matt, still using forward momentum, helped him toward the edge of the wharf, grabbing the gun and the back of the man's jacket as he let the dead weight fall over the edge and into the surf below leaving him alone on the deck with a new gun and the thugs jacket for disguise. Now he would just have to bluff his way into the building and hope he came up with a plan on the fly.

~

Matt hadn't settled from the brief encounter with the lookout before he could hear a vehicle pulling up in front of the building. Quickly donning his newfound jacket, he sauntered around to the front of the building as if he had just done his rounds and was expecting them. He positioned himself in front of the double doors that marked the entrance.

With one hand folded in front of the other Matt kept a grip on the Beretta which he semi-concealed under the front of the ex-guards jacket. With the Ruger tucked into his belt at the back for backup Matt took a stand to the right of the doors and stared straight ahead as if he had been expecting the carload of individuals.

The Lincoln Town Car pulled in right alongside the big red Peterbilt.

The two that crawled from the back of the car were obvious buyers. The thousand dollar suits really gave them away. They were way to slick for this neck of the woods. The other two dug themselves out of the front seat. It was more than obvious that this was the muscle. The two men were big enough to be four.

They were all bad business right down to the military haircuts. Matt didn't look sideways as the four passed and entered the building.

What he did do was move to his left as the door swung closed and used the heel of his boot to keep it from closing completely.

He didn't want the door to make a sound as he entered. Hopefully once inside the jacket would at least give him a moment where those inside would think that he was the previous owner and allow him enough time to assess the situation and move accordingly.

Matt slipped in giving the men from the car time to make their way to where the meeting was taking place at the back of the building. He stayed out of sight in the lobby of what looked to him like a makeshift American Legion.

From his vantage point, Matt could see a number of dart boards along the north wall and a lonely but well-used pool table occupied the other.

Matt heard a door closed farther back which he knew from his position under the open window outside was approximately where he had heard the voices of the smugglers and their buyers earlier.

Taking that as his cue to move, Matt silently made his way past the dartboards and the aging pool table, around a well-stocked bar that jutted out into the middle of the area from the south wall and up two risers of steps to a landing and a door. The door closed off the back of the building and was obviously where the men had congregated to do business judging by the rumble of male voices, muffled but distinguishable, coming from under it.

Matt listened intently, his ear pressed up against the door for a couple of minutes. He was trying to determine exactly how many men were in the room. He estimated eight but couldn't really be sure. He also knew that some if not all of them would be armed and they would not have gotten this far with the haul of ivory they had without some contingency plan. Some escape route out of this building beside the door that Matt was standing on the other side of. There was nothing he could do about that. He was alone and he was going to hope that the element of surprise pushed the odds in his favor.

So, that being said he would shoot the ones that went for a weapon, he would incapacitate those who did not and he would try to run down those who ran.

That was the best he could come up with in a pinch. It helped that he had the Ruger and the nifty little item he had pulled from the Asian assassins car wreck.

GET THE PARTY STARTED

When Matt entered the room there was no real reaction to his intrusion at first. The party might have been waiting for more guests and their initial lack of concern could have been just that.

As he quickly scanned the turned faces he didn't immediately recognize anyone. There was a small man standing near the back partially hidden by one of the bodyguards that he had just witnessed entering the building with the two suits.

A step to the left changed that and Matt found himself looking at a man who in international terrorist circles was a kingpin.

He was only known as Yuki Sato, a name in Japan that would be equivalent to John Smith in the United States. He had been linked to huge funding operations of everything from opium smuggling in China to financing ISIS operations in Syria. His organization did nothing small scale. Illegal transactions of billions of dollars had been tracked but never discovered in time to stop. His access to the best computer techs and hackers that money could buy always kept him one step ahead of the trackers.

Matt had only a moment to wonder what he was doing here on a dock in Connecticut for some transactions that would at best be a few million dollars.

"This man is not one of us." The man known as Yuki said calmly pointing in Matt's direction.

To a man, their hands went for their weapons.

The safety was already off on the Beretta under Matts' jacket and the first two rounds hit the bodyguards from the Town Car center mass and the third went through the neck of the man standing next to Sato.

Every man stopped in mid-reaction except Sato. He had strategically placed himself at the back of the room where a door leads out to the wharf and boat slips beyond. Using one of the other men in the room as cover he lunged for the door and was through it before Matt could stop him even though he fired off three more rounds taking out the cover man in the process.

There were still three men in the room left standing. Matt knew that if he had any hope of catching Yuki he would have to do something with them fast or let them go.

Matt didn't have any compunction about shooting or killing someone if they presented a real or imminent threat to his life. He did, however, make it a strict rule to not just gun someone down to expedite a situation.

"Gentlemen," Matt spoke softly. "Please turn around and put your hands behind your backs if you want to stay alive."

The men were quick to follow his demand and as soon as they did Matt used his pressure technique to put them all to sleep.

~

Matt jumped over the sleeping and the dead as he bolted for the door that Sato had escaped through. It had literally only been seconds since he had entered the room but as he exited out through the back door he knew he might be too late.

A boat was headed south in the Clinton harbor area and had already made some significant distance from the dock where Matt now stood. There were two ways to leave the harbor area. The first was out around the Cedar Island point. Once on the other side of the point, it was a straight run into the Long Island sound and anywhere for miles up and down the long island coast, North or South. The other was south into the Clinton river system that ran for miles to the north bordering the outskirts of town. This was the direction of the speeding boat.

There weren't many watercraft on the sound and what was there were sailboats. Keeled over in the east prevailing wind, their hulls slapping the light waves of the sound, they probably didn't even notice the speeding boat as it made a beeline for the river mouth.

Matt could only hope this was his target. The adjoining dock at the back of the complex was empty. That meant he would have to run to the slips that serviced the marina some four hundred feet away. It also meant that he would lose direct line of sight on the escaping boat.

There were only three boats tied up in the marina slips. Two were variations of personal fishing craft. Aluminum and around eighteen feet long. The third was a sleek twenty-foot ski boat. Bright red and yellow. If he could get it started, it wouldn't be inconspicuous but it looked fast.

Matt jumped down into the boat. He had already given his objective a good four-minute start. The Ruger was just the tool he needed to break the ignition switch off from the underside of the dashboard. He tore the three wires from the remaining switch, tied the red and purple together,

229

he then touched those to the remaining yellow wire. The first touch created a short burst of sparks which let him know the battery was not dead. The next touch he held long enough for the engine to turn over. The third got a roar from the starboard two hundred and sixty horsepower Mercruiser. He was in luck, the boat was fast and no one from the marina noticed his departure as he headed out into the sound and slammed the throttle forward, standing the boat on its tail as it struggled to get to plane.

Matt thought he could still see the other boat as it made the mouth of the river. He pointed the bow in that direction and took a minute to pull the cell phone out for a quick call.

"Well, Matt." The familiar voice was matter of fact. "Long time no hear. I can assume you are in need?"

"Yes," Matt replied. "I am in pursuit of someone I believe to be Yuki Sato." The surprised grunt on the other end of the call was the most reaction he had heard from his contact ever.

"Can you be sure? Our last intel tells us that Yuki Sato has gone underground and though his whereabouts are generally unknown it is assumed that he is hiding in Beijing."

"I hadn't heard that," Matt yelled back. It was getting

hard to hear and speak with the rushing wind and the roar of the engine. "I would like to say that I have seen the limited images available of him and I was standing about fifteen feet from someone who I would say met ninety percent of his profile. I can't tell you why he would be here in the U.S. because it looked for all intents and purposes to be just a bigger than usual ivory dump."

"Ok, well I'll trust your instincts. What is it you need?"

"Well, I did leave a bit of a mess in a big gray building at the end of the dock in Clinton, Connecticut. There are seven men there. Three are out for about another hour or so and four won't be going to school tomorrow. The other man I think is Yuki and I am in pursuit. I'm headed south toward the Clinton River in a red and yellow ski boat. Somehow I need eyes on him in case I don't catch up."

"Will get eyes on and let you know. Clean up is on its way. I'll get back to when we have the target. Then I want you to ditch that phone."

With that, the connection broke and Matt focused on getting the ski boat to the river mouth.

The boat flew and he made the turn into the

headwater of the river in time to see another craft ahead. It was a long way ahead but at least he would be able to catch it turning into any of the multitude of channels that connected to the river on either side.

Here the water was as smooth as glass and the ski boat picked up a couple more miles per hour. Matt trimmed the engine up just a bit to get as much out of it as he could. The distance between himself and the other craft was diminishing but not quickly enough.

Sato was smart. He wouldn't have made his escape route up this river if he didn't have a plan.

The phone in Matt's hand rang.

"There's a bridge about a mile and a half up from your position. We have the other boat under observation and there appears to be vehicle and man with binoculars focused down river waiting. This is most likely the point of egress. I can't get a car there in time for you to stay on his tail but I can get you in the air. Once you hit the bridge, go directly under it and you will see your ride. Toss the phone. You will be getting a new one."

With that, the line went dead and Matt concentrated on keeping as much speed up as he could.

HAYATO

Yuki Sato, born Hayato Adachi, got his first taste of trouble at the age of fifteen. His computer and math skills had led him down the wrong path and the dark side of the web had interested him more than simply playing war games and other mindless waists of time online.

He was fourteen when he made his first money hacking into some rich guys financials both on his personal computer and his financial institution and delivering the bank accounts and passwords to an unknown contractor who had paid him a large sum of money on completion.

He knew how to hide himself compromising the computer servers or networks owned by multi-level organizations. Using complicated stepping stone attacks, he would find inconsistencies in networks that would allow him to gain access and use their systems to hide whatever activity he needed to run while making it blend in with that server's general network activity.

Over a period of time, young Hayato found discrepancies in other systems through the ones he had already hacked and by the time he was fifteen he had a huge network of hidden resources from which he could accomplish almost anything.

Hayato by this time had already become Yuki Sato. That was his dark web handle. For six months Yuki had been making large sums of money from the resources he had found as he hacked his way through many big business and banking networks. Sometimes selling information to those looking to invade these institutions and sometimes, just for fun, crashing networks to see what would happen.

Maybe he had gotten cocky or maybe because he was so young he just made a mistake but on one of these just for fun crash events Yuki accidentally left a door open.

Authorities didn't exactly trace the IP address back to his computer but they did trace it to his home. Since he was living with his father, a well-known businessman in their town, they assumed that his dad was the culprit.

As they hauled his father from their home, all the while proclaiming his innocence, Yuki stood and watched him go with no remorse. He actually counted himself lucky and put it down as a lesson learnt.

The police searched the home for evidence but Yuki had at least known better than to keep the computer he used for his hacking under his bed, hidden under some loose floorboard in his room or tapped to the inside of the hearth they never used in the living room. No, his special laptop was hidden inside a hollowed out portion of a huge structural beam in the attic. In fact, he had so carefully constructed the hidey hole that even if you looked at it from above with a magnifying glass, even if you ran your hand down the beam neither would the latch open nor could you feel any point of entry. The latch itself could only be opened with a particular sound generated by his cell phone. It was so secure that if Yuki lost his phone he would not be able to get the laptop back without taking the beam out entirely.

He had been so careful with his preparation of the safe that he felt shame at having led the authorities to his home. He swore that would not happen again.

His father was eventually released when they realized he did not know enough about computers and hacking to have managed the intrusions that had collapsed the company's network.

When the police turned their investigation toward Yuki he stared down their pointed questions with an air of stupidity and answered them in broken sentences that eventually led them to believe he wasn't completely normal.

Yuki continued his hacking and left home two years later after amassing a small fortune in offshore accounts from his various illegal enterprises.

He hacked anything and everyone for a price. He even hacked the famous Yakuza or gokudō, taking large sums of money directly out of hidden accounts they owned around the globe.

He wasn't worried. They would never find him. He had made himself so well hidden with millions of IP possibilities upon millions of fake routings. It would take the most sophisticated algorithm a hundred years to source him out and even then, would it?

So Yuki Soto became a myth and a mystery. No one knew who he was or where he was, what he looked like or what he wanted. Over time the man himself became board. He had spent too much time behind a computer screen. He needed an adventure or at least some fresh air every now and then. His need to stretch his legs had taken him outside of his safety zone quite a few times in the last couple of years. Mostly since he had started securing money and hiding money for organizations even worse than the Yakuza. The Yakuza at least had a code. A standard that they lived by. These new clients cared for nothing. They took an ancient ideology and warped and mutilated it to suit their maniacal and bloodthirsty quest for power subjugating and humiliating their own people in the process not caring how many lay dead and murdered in their wake. Yuki had brokered many deals and hidden millions of dollars for these terrorist organizations and so thousands had lost their lives indirectly through the manipulations of Yuki Sato.

Still, the danger of it did spice things up.

It was the thrill of it and his urge to visit the United States that had led Yuki, at the ripe old age of twenty six, to a dock in Connecticut with his two paid bodyguards dead and subsequently into a speedboat that he had conveniently tied up in a slip behind the place he was going to observe an ivory sale. He had never forgotten the lesson he had learned at the age of fifteen. He always had an escape plan.

What no one knew was that Yuki had been found out. The Yakuza didn't take kindly to someone hacking and stealing from them and they weren't just a gang of thugs either. They had their own well trained and equally brilliant computer wizards. They laid traps for Yuki in their banking transactions but after a couple of years of trying to track the young hacker, they were no closer to finding out who it was. They finally just got lucky.

One of the younger Yakuza programmers, a woman, had been out at a club frequented by many underground hackers and cyberpunks and had encountered a very mysterious and sullen young man at the bar. She had seen him a couple of times in the place and finally asked the bartender if he knew who he was. The bartender commented that the guy came in a couple of times a week, kept to himself and usually get pretty loaded. He had never seen him with or talk to anyone. One thing he observed was that the person drank expensively. The Chivas Regal he was drinking was six hundred a shot.

She was more than interested in the young man. Not just because he was obviously rich but he wasn't bad looking either.

Her first encounter with Yuki Sato was not very productive. He seemed depressed and barely grunted at her when she tried to start up a conversation. His rebuff of her only sparked her hacker spirit. It was a puzzle to be solved and as anyone should know you never leave a puzzle laying around when there is a nerd in the room.

Over the next few months the young Yakuza programmer, her name was Mika, periodically ran into Yuki and tried to make a connection. Her persistence paid off to the extent that he began to talk to her. It was weird, she thought. She knew that she was a good looking woman but Yuki didn't seem to react to her femininity. Even when she would drop subtle sexual hints, he just ignored them.

She had learned that he was a programmer. Not because he had told her but because he hadn't. He had said that his name was Hayato Adachi probably assuming that it would have been a name no one would recognize and that he was a businessman. When she pressed him on what company he worked for he told her he was an independent contractor.

That sent up red flags immediately. The only independent contractors she knew of that made enough money to drink six hundred dollars a shot scotch worked for her bosses and they weren't really businessmen.

Hayato's unwillingness to engage with her in anything more than superficial chatter got her thinking.

Mika started to look for Hayato online. Her bosses frowned on using their systems for personal use but her interest had been piqued.

It took a couple of weeks but she finally found a police article in a small town newspaper that mentioned a businessman with the last name Adachi. It recalled the arrest of a certain Itaru Adachi for cyber theft and hacking. It was later learned that Itaru was not the criminal and released. What caught

Mika's attention was the article went on to mention the questioning of a son who was underage and could not be mentioned.

Could this be Hayato?

A week later, after another frustrating encounter with the moody young man at the club, Mika decided to follow him when he left the bar. At least if she saw where he lived it might give her some insight into why he was so withdrawn.

She watched as Hayato left the club? Her intent was to let him get outside and then get to the door in time to pick up his trail outside. What she had not expected was to see a man, a bodyguard judging from his size and demeanor, get up from a table at the back of the club and follow Hayato out.

She bolted for the door expecting them to wait for valet service but she was surprised again to see that they were met by a large town car and a driver.

The bodyguard held the door for Hayato and then wedged himself into the front seat. There was no opportunity for her to follow this night but she would be prepared the next time she encountered Hayato Adachi.

Ten days later Mika saw Hayato again at the club. This time she didn't waste any time trying to get close to him.

She watched as he drowned his sorrows, whatever they might be, and then left before he had finished his last drink.

She had brought her Kawasaki Ninja motorbike and was waiting a block down from the club when Hayato and his bodyguard exited.

Mika's job with the Yakuza was a desk job but she was not without other skills. That was one of the reasons she had been accepted into a gang that was predominantly male. One of her favorite things was her motorcycle. She wasn't just a good rider, she was a great rider.

This night, lights off, she tailed Hayato's car with his two bodyguards to an amazing Koyoto home about ten miles from the club. It sat in the middle of a park-like piece of property that must have cost a fortune. She was more intrigued than ever. If he was a programmer, he must be a hell of a good one to live in such luxury.

The next day, Mika talked to her boss, who was a wakagashira or first lieutenant and told him about Hayato. Her tale piqued the man's interest and he passed the information along to those who would decide if it was worth investigating. That information got passed up the line to the oyabun who thought it was worthy of further investigation.

It took a year of very secretive and careful surveillance of Hayato's movements, meetings, and any Wi-Fi or digital signal they could get their hands on, to make the gang almost positive of who they were dealing with.

The oyabun finally issued an order to have Hayato kidnapped. It was a simple thing as kidnapping was a part of everyday business in the Yakuza. Ransoming those they kidnapped stood for almost forty-five percent of their yearly income.

They knew where Hayato liked to drink so they just waited outside for the boy his bodyguard to come out. They had paid off the valet and one of the group took his place. When the two passed the fake valet, gave the bodyguard a gentle tap behind the ear with the butt of his gun, others grabbed Hayato, flinging him into a waiting car then all three disappeared into the crowded club before Hayato's driver could even react.

Hayato's interrogation by the Yakuza boss was brief. He might have been a world-renowned hacker and programmer but he was still a boy and scared shitless. When threatened with the loss of a couple of pinky fingers and something else that would leave him walking funny for the rest of his life, which might, according to the boss, only be a few minutes long, Hayato, or as they knew him to be Yuki Sato, gave up the goods so to speak.

Basically, Yuki spilled his guts. When the oyabun heard Yuki's story he quickly realized that not only was he going to get all the Yakuza money back that Yuki had stolen but he was also going to get millions maybe billions from Yuki's vast database and offshore accounts.

Luckily for Yuki, he would get to keep all his digits and his unit while working permanently for the Yakuza gang who had taken him hostage. He was now a Yakuza man. In for life with no way out.

Now as he flew along an unknown river on the coast of the U.S. the adrenalin made him laugh out loud. It was crazy. He had not seen the frantic scene in the dockside building as he was directly behind one of the bodyguards but he had heard the gunshots and the thud of bodies hitting the floor as he sprinted out the back door and he could imagine what had taken place.

"How smart I am," he thought "to have had an escape plan."

Yuki would have been smarter to have taken a look behind him at the speeding ski boat gaining ground.

It wouldn't quite get to him in time to catch him but it would have maybe given him a little wake-up call for assuming he had everything figured out.

THE CHASE

Matt could see that he wouldn't be catching Yuki. He hoped that whatever TUSC had planned it involved tracking the mysterious hacker until Matt could catch up. This was one target that would make a difference. If Matt could stop or permanently end Yuki's contribution in the world of Terrorism which directly corresponded to the imminent extinction of the elephant, he could safely say that he had done some good in the world.

That had always been he and his mentor, Ethan's, intent. To use his hard-earned skill and foresight to take down the criminal enterprises that threatened the world. To source out those who would use the innocent and unaware to manipulate governments and oppress populations to their own criminal and illegal gains and to shut down their revenue streams by any means possible.

Matt had had other successes in the past but they all paled with the dent taking down Yuki Soto would put in the ivory trade and the funding of a couple of very big terrorist organizations.

From where he stood behind the windshield of the racing ski boat, it was hard for Matt to tell exactly what kind of car Yuki had gotten into after he had docked the boat up ahead. It was just too far away to say anything other than it was black.

He would follow the plan. TUSC had said to go past the dock and under the bridge and he would get him airborne.

It was a couple of minutes after the escaping Soto had slammed into the dock with the getaway boat before Matt reached the spot. It wasn't like it was isolated or anything there was a First Liberty Bank just on the edge of the highway and the launch area where he had dumped the boat and gotten into his waiting car. There was also a marina across the river from that point as well but Matt didn't have time to track down someone in the sparsely populated landings to see if someone had seen a black car or got a license plate he could track down.

Matt kept going right past the landings and under the bridge.

As he popped out the other side he was greeted by the whooshing blades of a black Bell 525 Relentless helicopter idling on the bank of the small inlet that hugged the far side of the bridge.

Matt beached the stolen boat and ran to the chopper. The door popped open as he reached its side and grabbing the door handle he swung himself in. The pilot was familiar.

"Long time, no see sailor," Matt wasn't shocked that it was Marianna, the pilot who had helped him out of a couple of tight situations back in Duala and got him into a couple on the flight back to the U.S. after he had escaped.

"You're like a magician's rabbit, popping up whenever a little assistance is needed to finish a magic trick." Matt flipped back.

"I think I did a bit more than a little in Africa don't you?" Marianna replied.

"This is a pretty big chopper." Matt changed the subject, is there a shower in the back?"

He could see by her smile that Marianna found the humor in it.

"Do we have eyes on?? Matt asked.

"Yes, but I'm not sure of a course of action. TUSC is leaving it up to you, or should I say us, to come up with something."

Well, the first thing is let's get this thing in the air. Then we can try to figure something out."

"There is a shower in the back." Marianna laughed.

Matt checked over his shoulder. This was no ordinary chopper. The back of it looked like a friggin hotel room.

"Better concentrate on the getaway car," Matt said.

"Party pooper." Marianna grinned back.

Marianna brought the huge turbine up to full speed and got the chopper airborne. Once she had attained a critical altitude, the helicopter nosed down and started to pick up speed.

"I'm going to give the highway a wide birth. Don't want them to notice us tailing them."

Marianna spoke while handing Matt a Polaris monocular with a twenty-time magnification and a two-way earbud.

"Once we're at altitude, dump the phone. TUSC is going to call the sat feed to you as we fly."

Matt was surprised that there was so much communication going on. Typically he was left to his own devices. This was far and beyond any support he had had in the last couple of years.

Marianna had taken the chopper approximately ten miles to the west of the highway and to about five thousand feet. They were nose down and heading south back toward the city.

Matt knew if Yuki got back to the city he would be lost. Once he could connect to contacts in New York they would secrete him away and he would be lost. This was a once in possibly a lifetime chance to take down the biggest money launderer and financial contributor to the world of terrorism in history. Matt wasn't about to let that happen.

Matt tapped the earpiece and waited.

"Still got the cell phone?" the voice in Matt's ear queried.

"Yup," Matt responded.

"What altitude are you at? Matt looked at Marianna and asked the same question.

"Five thousand." He said.

"Toss the phone." the voice commanded. "Preferably over water if you can. If you can't, the woods."

Matt slid the small side window built into the main window jam of the passenger cockpit area open and flipped the phone out. They weren't over water but from the altitude they were at, there wouldn't be much left of the plastic phone.

"Subject vehicle is heading south on I95, they are

observing the speed limit. They may think that no one is following." The voice on the earbud had changed. Matt thought it might be the sat feed controller.

"Got it," Matt replied. "What's our distance?"

"Approximately fifteen mikes northwest. Sending sat feed to your heads up display."

With that, the heads up virtual feed appeared in the windshield of the chopper. The satellite was zeroed in, the black car no longer staying within the speed limit, the heads up had it clocked at over one hundred miles an hour.

"Pull the satellite feedback ten k," Matt asked. Immediately the view on the heads up pulled back and gave Matt a wide view of the speeding car and the surrounding area.

Matt could see for miles. The car would soon be heading into the outskirts of Bridgeport. He hoped that the game plan for Soto was to get back to New York and disappear. The drive to the city would give Matt the opportunity to formulate a plan.

As he studied the road ahead, Matt thought he might just have the solution. Just south of Bridgeport, he could see a new construction area. Homes being constructed on either side of the highway were accessed from a side road that did not require an overpass. At any time, the crossing would be dangerous. Matt hoped for Sato it would be deadly.

Only feet away, concealed by a large stand of white oak was an open lot large enough to land a chopper the size of the Bell. In the real-time feed from the satellite, Matt could see some heavy construction and earth moving equipment that just might do the job he had in mind.

Matt rolled out his plan to Marianna over the mouthpiece built into the flight helmet he was wearing.

"Might work." She said. "Best to get down there and see if you can get one of those machines running."

The other end of the sat feed broke in. Matt had forgot they would hear his conversation with Marianna.

"If you can get one of those Caterpillar scrapers running we can time your entry to the highway so that the subject will have no way to escape. We can time it so they have no recourse but to stop or broadside the scraper."

"Let me get down there and see if I can gain access

to what we need. If I don't we'll have to wait to get airborne again and come up with something else."

Marianna punched the throttle on the helo and Matt started to go over his plan in his mind. Seemed simple enough but there was always something. If they timed it right they could get to the construction site unseen and Matt would have time to commandeer one of the heavy earth moving machines. Then it would be up to those watching overhead to put the critical timing in place.

~

Martin Cech was feeling pretty lucky these days. He had found steady work as a heavy equipment operator ever since he had migrated from the Czech Republic to the United States seven years ago. This new job in Connecticut looked like it would be the best one yet. The community plan for the forty thousand homes was ten years. That was enough work for him to get a new car. What a joy that would be to dump the piece of shit 2002 Toyota Avalon he had been using for the last five years and get a brand new Ford F150. He had been drooling over brochures and TV ads for over a year now and he knew exactly the options and color he wanted.

Back home in the Czech Republic, one could only afford a new American built truck if you worked for the government or were a criminal. Both positions hated by the people. The first, for their oppression and robbery of the everyday working class that kept them in their fancy suits and cars and the second, for the exact same thing. The only difference was that if you were a working-class stiff in the Czech Republic you probably had more than one criminal in the family.

In Martin's world, there was more than a couple in the family. He was a hard worker. He worked forty hours a week for a state-owned company as a pipe fitter. A skill he inherited from his father who had worked as a skilled laborer for an independent plumbing company before he died in a car accident in 2007 prompting Martin Junior's immigration to the U.S.

More than once, Martin had been propositioned by a relative to join one of the many Balkan organized crime groups involved in gambling, casinos, drug trafficking or even cigarette smuggling.

With his father's passing, Martin knew the requests to join one of these criminal enterprises would only get more aggressive, so after researching and communicating with an employer in the States, he had his prospective employer file a petition to bring him to the U.S. That was eventually approved by the Immigration services and he immediately applied for a work visa.

Martin had been working as a heavy equipment operator for most of his time in America. The new job with Westport Construction was a dream come true and as he made his way to the lot that held the D9's and the Caterpillar scrapers, he couldn't have imagined the way this day would turn into a story for his grandchildren.

AMERICAN BUILT

The Bell 525 Relentless screamed into the clearing adjacent to the compound that held the bulk of Westport Constructions heavy earth moving equipment. Matt was out of the chopper and at the gate of the compound in about sixty seconds. There were no guards or security. The compound was simply cordoned off with a ten foot high linked fence and an access door that stood open leaving Matt easy access to the huge machinery.

It was simple for Matt, he just picked the biggest dirt hauler in the place and jumped up onto the driver side steps and hauled the door open.

"Hey man!" a voice behind Matt made him glance over his shoulder. "That is no toy and I don't think you want to screw with it."

Matt saw a blonde man mid-forties staring up at him with his hands on his hips. Matt didn't have time for this. He jumped into the driver seat and closed the door. One look at the dashboard in the big earth mover and Matt knew one thing for sure. He was going to need a lesson in just turning the thing on.

Matt opened the door and yelled down to the man

still standing below staring up at him.

"How do you start this thing?" he inquired.

"You don't." the man said.

"I don't have time to explain right now but you will be doing your country a great service if you tell me how to start this thing."

"I am new to this country." The man replied with a bit of a grin.

"Please," Matt begged. "It is truly a matter of life or death."

"And it would be a matter of my job and so my life if I tell you." The man replied.

"You are certainly right about one thing," Matt replied pulling the Berretta and pointing it at the surprised man on the ground. "So get up here and be assured I will shoot you if you feel the urge to screw around."

Martin didn't need to be asked twice. He had often encountered guns in his homeland. More than once in his family home and he knew better than to try and be sneaky when someone was pointing one at you.

Martin climbed the access rungs on the side of the Caterpillar and slid into the seat.

The Cat 627K was a technically advanced designed scraper but with only one seat and the close proximity to a gun-wielding man didn't make Martin very comfortable.

"Please trust me," Matt spoke to the obviously agitated worker. "I don't want you or I to get hurt or worse killed here but I need you to do what I tell you to do. It's going to sound crazy but that's just the way it is."

Matt could hardly imagine what this maniac had in mind. He could only think that at least he had forty-two feet and almost eighty tons of machinery underneath him for protection from whatever this lunatic wanted to do.

It was at this point that Matt got a transmission from Marianna in the chopper.

"Ok Matt, heads up from the sat feed. The target is enroute. We have an issue with your plan. There is some traffic in the area. Could result in collateral damage."

"I had to ask for assistance to drive this thing. Can you think of another option?" Matt replied.

"Is your assistant a willing participant?"

"No." Matt responded."

"Maybe, I'm going to get airborne and see if I can distract the target and scare off the traffic at the same time."

"Don't scratch the shower." Matt shot back.

"Satcom is going to give you your start point. Good luck."

"Thanks, you too."

"Time to get this thing rolling," Matt informed his assistant.

Marianna got the chopper back up to speed and in the air. This time there was no keeping out of site. She wanted the fleeing vehicle to spot her and to know her intent. As the helo screamed back along I95, she stayed just high enough to make an impression as she passed travelers north and south on the freeway.

Ten minutes out, she passed the black sedan hurrying south and spun the chopper around in pursuit. The tail rotor screeching with the effort.

Those in the car could not mistake her maneuver for anything but a tactical pursuit.

Marianna came up behind the speeding car and stayed about four hundred yards back but just high enough to avoid common traffic. She wanted to send the criminals a message. Sitcom's had confirmed that this was the target and as soon as the chopper took up its position behind the car the driver hit the gas while the occupant in the passenger side took the opportunity to lean out the window and take a few shots in her direction. Marianna was close enough to see that the person hanging out the window was Asian. Probably Soto. Soto was a legendary computer hacker and money launderer but she had never heard anything about his ability with a gun. Still better to take evasive action than to have some punk with a gun get a lucky shot in.

Marianna kept the helo close but randomly slid the bird from side to side, mostly staying on the drive side until the man with the gun had to climb part way out to get a shot, then she would slip back the other way until he had to almost cross himself to get a bearing on her.

The ruse was working. The getaway car was now traveling at a very high rate of speed and the occupants were more concerned with the helicopter that dogged them than keeping a constant eye on the road.

Marianna tapped her earpiece.

"Ok guys, I have the target distracted. As far as I can see upcoming traffic is minimal and the chopper is helping keep those off the highway ahead. I will stay in position till you stop them unless they get a lucky shot off. Matt, I'm turning you over to the satellite team. They're going to call it from here."

"Got it," Matt replied. "Thanks for the help."

With that, the chopper broke contact and Matt had the driver take the Caterpillar out of the compound and out onto the access road that intersected the highway between the two housing developments.

Matts headset came to life.

"Ok Matt, ask the guy you commandeered what the top speed of that thing is and how long it takes to get it up to top speed."

"Hey," Matt looked at the man in the driver's seat of the Cat. "My guys want to know the top speed of this thing and how long it takes to get up to that speed."

"I know it has a top speed of thirty-three miles an hour according to the manual. I never really thought about how long it took to get it up to that speed. I'm gonna guess maybe forty-five seconds. I have to tell you I don't think I have ever driven it that fast before."

"Don't worry about that. Just make sure when I tell you to stand on that gas pedal and keep it down till I tell you to stop."

"Got it," Martin replied. He didn't sound like he was having fun.

"Did you guys get that?" Matt asked into the air.

"We did. Just extrapolating the distance you would have to travel to make that speed, and an impact scenario."

Matt didn't really like the sound of "impact scenario" but he was too far in and out of ideas.

He turned to the man he had held at gunpoint.

"What's your name?" He asked.

"Martin." Martin just stared out the window.

"Well Martin, You're not going to like this but I have no choice. I am chasing some really bad men. Unfortunately for you, now you are too."

"That's just great," Martin replied. "I left my country to get away from this shit and I end up right in the middle of it."

"Your accent. Serb, Czech, Pole?"

"Czech." Martin gave up.

"I spent some time in your country." Matt offered.
261

"Some beautiful parts and some not so nice."

"Yes. I got out because the not so nice parts were closing in on me. Ironic, isn't it?"

The conversation was interrupted by the sat team.

"Ok, you're going to need about four hundred feet to get that thing up to speed. You have to stay on the gas until you get to the southbound edge of the highway and then slam on the brakes. The skid should take you into perfect position."

"And if it doesn't?" Mat queried.

"Good question."

Shit, Matt thought.

"Ok, Martin, here we go. We need to get this thing about four hundred feet from the edge of the highway there and when I tell you to, punch it. I need you to get this thing going as fast as you can until we reach the southbound edge of the pavement and then slam on the brakes. I have to tell you we are trying to stop a speeding car and we won't have time to abandon this rig before it hits. I think this thing is big enough that we should be ok but it's still going to be one hell of an impact."

"That's just great." Mating replied. "I was just getting happy about this job and then you came along. Probably get my visa revoked over this."

"I can assure you. You won't be losing anything if we get out of this unscathed." Matt promised.

"Oh, that makes me feel really good." Martin had been working on his American sarcasm and he thought that one was pretty good.

They pulled the Caterpillar down the access road to approximately four hundred feet and waited.

They didn't wait long. Martin had just put the rig in neutral when Matt said: "get ready."

To this point, Martin hadn't really been too concerned. The guy with the gun didn't sound like some desperado. The fact that he obviously had outside resources helping him made it sound almost legit. He thought it might even be one of those crazy reality shows he sometimes watched on Tuesday night. Now he wished he had made a run for it.

"Ok, hit it," Matt yelled in his ear.

Too late for regrets, Martin thought as he pushed the pedal to the floor and began running the gears up to their max before shifting to the next.

~

The Cat came sliding to a halt in the middle of the

highway just in time to have the black sedan carrying Yuki Sato, the driver and one other bodyguard at a speed in excess of one hundred and forty miles an hour into the side of the orange scraper.

The impact was as Matt had mentioned substantial. If the car had hit the Cat closer to the rear axle, it might not have had much significance to Matt and Martin but it had made contact closer to the front of the scraper.

Since the cab was connected to the scraper by a central hinge point, the force jackknifed the cab throwing the cab door on Matt's side open, spilling Matt and Martin onto the pavement.

The drop was a few feet and since Martin had been sitting in the driver's seat, he had been ejected second. The lesser of two evils because he ended up landing on top of Matt breaking his fall but winding Matt in the process.

As Matt lay gasping, Martin high tailed it for the refuge of the compound to call the police.

Matt was banged up a bit but he quickly regained his breath and pulled himself to his feet beside what remained of the getaway car.

Matt had never seen anything like it. The impact had literally compacted the metal so it looked like what was left of the body sat over top of duel wheels. The front axle had broken free and the rear axle had been forced so far forward that it looked like some kind of carnival ride, one almost touching the other.

Matt moved to the front where the driver had been ejected through the windshield and into the side of the Cat. He had impacted so hard that it looked like he had poked his head through the side of the scraper to see what was in there. His jacket and shirt had been torn off and were stuck to the side of the Cat thankfully covering the area where his head should have been. Matt could see even through the blood that his entire back was tattooed in the Yakuza style with a huge dragon, the reds of the tongue and claws blending into the bloodied body.

The passenger was still in the car but Matt could tell by the kink in his neck that he would not be traveling any further, ever.

Then Matt noticed something incredible. Sato, or at least who he assumed was Sato, had part of an arm and a hand sticking out from under the dashboard and the back of the front seats which had slammed forward with the sudden stop so that they looked like they were part of the dash.

He must have been in the back seat and the impact had thrown him up into the front of the car and under the dash. There was no way in hell he could have survived the crash but as Matt pulled open the driver's door, he could see that the set of legs belonging to the body under the dash was wrapped up over what remained of the console and then forced back under the dash on the driver's side by the seat as it tore off its bolts to the chassis and was forced forward by the trunk trying to kiss the firewall.

As he stared, Matt caught a quick tremor in one of the fingers of the hand sticking out beside the body that was still strapped into the passenger seat. If you didn't look closely you would think the arm belonged to that body. It was, in fact, connected to the person jammed under the dash.

Just then, the Bell landed on the pavement fifty feet from the wreck. Matt turned in its direction to see Marianna climbing down from the cockpit props still turning. He also noticed the traffic building up behind the chopper. It was getting busy.

"Let's go," Marianna called as she drew nearer.

"There's one alive I think. Might be Sato." Matt yelled back. If it's him and he is alive I want to take him in."

"We have about two minutes before shit hits the fan here Matt. So if you can get him out in time great. If not, we're out of here."

Matt ran to the other side of the car and pulled the crumpled passenger door open. Now he could see how someone might end up under the dashboard and possibly survive that kind of crash.

It was Sato and he must have been sent flying by the initial impact. As he entered the front seat his inertia had been slowed by the bodies of the two in the front seat. Their inevitable end had been slowed just enough by seatbelts so that Sato had slammed into their backs and then dropped down between the passengers in the front and as the body of the vehicle crushed forward was pushed under the dashboard possible saving his life.

Once Matt had the door open he pulled the dead passenger out and literally threw him on the ground. Then he reached under what was the front of the passenger seat but was jammed up under the dash so that the only space left there was that which was occupied by the body of Sato.

Matt used all his strength and what leverage he could get from the warped framework of the car to tear the mangled front passenger seat out. It came away with some coaxing the already compromised bolts holding on for one last second.

He couldn't tell if Sato was alive or dead but one thing for sure was he was a mess. His right arm, the

267

one that had the telltale twitch was torn out of the socket at the shoulder and turned around backward. Matt grabbed onto what was left of his jacket and pulled. The dead weight came sliding out of the car. It looked like a snake slithering over a pile of rocks.

There must be a lot of broken bones in there. Matt thought.

He was out of time. He picked up the broken body and ran for the chopper.

The side door stood open and he unceremoniously tossed Sato's limp body in.

Matt still had one foot on the ground when the bell lifted off. Marianna was in a hurry.

"Police are ninety seconds out. Hold on."

With that, the helo nosed done and took off with a force that set Matt back in his seat and tossed the body in the back around like a rag doll.

They were quickly out over open water and heading back toward New York. Matt had a moment to wonder where Martin had gotten off to. He didn't get a chance to thank him. He would make sure he found him out and get that message to him.

NO NEED FOR TORTURE

When the State police got to the crash scene they at first were wondering what the hell a giant earth moving machine was doing in the middle of the highway. They had arrived from the Norwalk side of the event where they had been called to an incident at the Maritime Aquarium.

It wasn't until they walked around to the north side of the Caterpillar that they understood what all the frantic phone calls had been about.

If this hadn't been a compact car when it came off the assembly line it sure as hell was now.

There was one body splayed out on the ground next to the passenger's side. It looked like maybe the passenger seat along with its occupant had been flung from the vehicle on impact.

Officer James Baldwin's partner Mick Jacobs worked his way around to the driver's side. He probably would have been ok with the sight of the ejected body if he hadn't of lifted the remnants of the jacket and shirt.

When he was done puking he told Jimmy it was a site that he would never get out of his brain.

After a quick perusal of the interior of the car, the officers noticed at least two guns in the mess. That along with witnesses talking about a big black helicopter landing on the highway and taking off with one of the bodies prompted them to get a hold of the FBI field office in Bridgeport. Their brief report got a couple of agents scrambling and a command to secure the perimeter of the site and anything they thought relevant to the scene until they got there.

~

Marianna and Matt where miles south by then, their destination, a little chunk of concrete just off the side of runway 31 on the far north end of JFK International.

"That was pretty intense." Matt broke the silence.

"Where did the guy go you coerced into driving that thing for you?" Marianna wanted to know.

"I don't know," Matt replied. "But I hope he went home and pretended he was never there. That's what I would do."

"I call bullshit on that's what you would do. Why don't you check the sack of bones you got in the back and see if he's dead or not?"

Matt had almost forgot about what was left of Sato lying face down in the back of the chopper. In the rush to get away he was more concentrated on leaving the scene and trying to flush the adrenaline from his system than he was on whether or not Sato was alive.

Matt unbuckled and moved into the back of the helo. Sato's broken form lay in an expanding puddle of blood and ooze. Some his and some his ex-partners.

When Matt flipped him over, he was pretty hard to look at. The right side of his skull looked like a softball sized something had made a dint in it. His arms and legs were crooked in too many ways. Most of his teeth were gone and his nose was about as flat as you could get without having it look like you had no nose.

Matt reached down and stuck a couple of fingers against his neck. He was more than a little bit surprised to feel a faint pulse. Not that he gave a shit whether Sato lived or died because he was a lot closer to the dead side than the live but he thought, if there was a chance the bag of broken bones could give them some information on other lines of finance for organizations like Isis and Hezbollah, he would likely do so without the usual threat of torture. By the look of him, if he did survive, he would likely give up the info just to get some pain medication.

271

Matt would soon find out that he needn't have worried whether Sato lived or died. The poor bastard would give up his secrets either way.

THE TALE IS IN THE TAT

The Bell 525 Relentless screamed south toward JFK International and the concrete testing and training area at the furthest end of the complex.

The space was used for testing and training pilots and emergency response teams. It even contained a sixty-foot pool that boasted a submerged 727 fuselage for water landing and submerged rescue training.

As they approached the landing pad the headsets crackled and a voice instructed them to land at the far end of the concrete pad where a forty-five-foot motorhome stood waiting.

Marianna wheeled the big chopper around so that the passenger side faced the RV and the vacant road and storage area beyond.

Matt swung down from his seat, slid the back door of the helo open and unceremoniously grabbed what was left of Yuki Sato by the back of the shirt and the belt around his pants and hauled him out and into the open door of the motorhome.

As he struggled up the steps he was met by a man followed by a woman both dressed in hospital blues. The man reached down and grabbed Sato under the

273

arms proceeded to help Matt carry him to a waiting operating table.

The interior of the RV was expansive. The center of the bus had been cleared away to accommodate an operating theater that would have been the envy of many hospitals.

Matt sat down on a bench seat outside the operating area but still within eyesight. He wanted to be there if Sato regained consciousness or if there was anything the doctor could tell him that might further his cause. He was still a bit nerved up after the chase and its explosive end and he found his legs wouldn't keep still while he sat and watch the two medics work over the body.

~

Matt could hear the chopper taking off as he sat and stared into space. He wondered if the cleanup crew had any problems with the mess in Clinton. He was fairly certain that that many gunshots would have been noticed by someone. He also wondered if they had found the cache of ivory. It must have been in one of the other rooms while the men were negotiating price and delivery.

Suddenly Matt heard one of the medics speak in a very surprised voice. "What the hell?"

He jumped up and went to the table where the medics had begun to cut the clothing off the unconscious body. He had been laying on his back so they had just taken a pair of razor-sharp surgical scissors and cut his clothes off right down the middle including the pant legs. When they rolled him over was when they discovered the bizarre tattooing.

Matt knew immediately what it was. He had seen this before in Japan. The Yakuza would force their accountants, pimps, drug runners and anyone connected to them who provided a service to have the names, safe houses, bank accounts, password or any other pertinent information pertaining to their particular position in the organization intricately woven into a traditionally styled tattoo. Always in code, so no one could decipher the meaning and so intertwined into the fabric of the tattoo, it would take someone who knew what they were looking for to see it.

Sato's tattoo was beautiful. The huge Komodo dragon covered his entire back even allowing his legs to become the legs and tail of the serpent.

What had brought the medics exclamation was sheer coincidence.

He had been examining the softball-sized dent in Sato's skull and had was using a digital magnifying lens to bring the injury to a big screen monitor for better observation. As they removed the clothes and turned the body over the lens had been jarred so that it now pointed mid back on the subject. What was so astonishing was where the tattoo was brought into magnified focus on screen one could see that the lines and fill coloring were actually made up of tiny zero's and one's so small they would not have been immediately noticeable by the human eye.

Sato must have been tracked down by the Yakuza and instead of killing him for his hacking of their network and the theft of millions of dollars, they had given him an option. Join the gang or become fish food.

It was obvious which one he took.

Matt had encountered a number of these tattoos while he trained in Japan. Master Tsuneko had told him of this practice and shown him a number of photographs of such tattoos. Because he had seen these photos Matt had even seen one in real life at a traditional Japanese bathhouse where it was clear the person with the tattoo must have believed there would be no one there that could identify his special markings other than they were Yakuza.

The Master explained the gravity and the purpose for them. This was the Yakuza's way of binding their minions to their gang. The men who had these tattoos knew that outside the protection of the Yakuza they would be hunted men. Not just from rival gangs but from every law enforcement agency in the world looking for insight into the workings of the secretive gang.

One thing for sure, Matt had never seen anything as intricate as this one. He would need extensive photos of the artwork.

Just then, Sato gave a long sigh. Matt looked at the doctor.

The doctor just looked back and shook his head. "I did a quick body scan and I don't see any bones that aren't broken or shattered." He said.

With that, he slapped an x-ray of Yuki's entire midsection into a clip above one of the RV windows.

"What am I looking at doc?" Matt questioned.

"See these white areas?" The doctor said pointing to what looked like balloon shaped areas that ran the length of the right side of Yuki's body. Matt just nodded.

"That is empty space. It's supposed to be where all his vital organs are. But they have been jammed with such force to the right that they have denigrated. He's gone. That was just gas expelling from his

277

internal bleeding and ruptured intestines."

Matt couldn't help but feel a little bad for Sato but he was already trying to figure out what to do next.

They needed high-resolution images of every segment of the tattoo and if Sato had been on Yakuza business at the Clinton pier they would be looking for him if not right now pretty damn quick.

"What kind of imaging system do you have on board?" Matt asked the physician.

"Best you can get. We have a sixteen-megapixel camera and 4k video."

"Let's do both and let's do it now. What about the internet? Do you have secure feeds?"

"The satellite is secure to one destination." The doc supplied. "You can clear it with the phone on the dash."

Matt made his way to the driver's seat and picked up the cell phone that was sitting in the dash tray.

He immediately recognized TUSC's voice. "Whada ya got?" TUSC wasn't wasting words.

"I need to send some photos ASAP. If it is what I think it is I need to do it now and then get the hell out of here." Matt replied.

"Ok," TUSC replied. "The sat feed is secured to us. Do it and then get the bus rolling. I'll check the pics and get you clear."

Matt turned to see the two medics looking at him. He gave them the thumbs up and then took a quick look around the huge diameter of the training center. Nothing twigged so he secured the door to the RV and went back to check on the photos.

"The photos are on their way." The woman said. "We're just about done with the video, so give us two minutes and you can start this bus rolling."

"Any weapons on board?" Matt wondered out loud.

"The wall in the hall between the bathroom and the rear bedroom door. Push it in, it'll pop out."

Matt moved pass the two and made his way to the back of the RV.

The wall popped open just as described. Behind the secret door was an arsenal. There were two Glock's a Smith and Wesson and .45 ACP Colt. Along with these handguns was a Makarov a Remington 700, and a couple of hand grenades.

Matt had left the handy little Beretta in the chopper so he grabbed one of the Glock's and the grenades and hurried back up front to the driver's seat and started the motor home.

"Time to move." He shouted to the back.

"All locked in." came the reply.

Matt hit the accelerator and headed for the end of the cement training area closest to where the RV had been parked. He could see there was access to a roughly paved road that might get them out to the four-lane boulevard that circumvented the airport.

The phone on the dash rang. Matt hit the answer button as he wheeled the big RV onto the service road and headed for the open boulevard.

"I'm watching your progress on satellite. See the three red service buildings? Straight past them and head for the cement abutment that is blocking your path to the boulevard. Don't worry, it's only painted to look like concrete. It's really heavy rubber so it'll get a bit bumpy but you'll get to the highway. You can only go north but I'll get you turned around. As soon as you hit the road, get rid of Sato. He's got tracking on him. You might want to step on it. Incoming far end of that service road.

Matt stood on it. The RV handled like a bus. Top heavy and sluggish but its sheer weight took the fake blockade out with nothing more than a bump that the huge vehicle's suspension took in stride.

He got the motorhome, headed north and had only gone a mile when he pulled the big tub into a grassed area just past the end of runway 22. On any given day, the lot would be populated with jet watchers. The field was situated very close to the end of the runway and was a perfect observation point to watch big jets coming and going.

Today the area had only one vehicle parked facing the runway. That was a good thing. Matt wheeled the RV to the end of the field where there was a small outcropping of scrub and four or five closely grouped tamarack trees.

He pulled the bus up close to the trees and hit the brakes.

"Get him off the table and help me get him out of here." He yelled down to the medics belted into their seats in the back.

The male medic jumped to it and between the two of them, they got what was left of Sato out of the RV and hidden in the scrub and brush that surrounded the outcropping of trees.

"Get back in the bus," Matt ordered. When the medic got back on the RV Matt lifted Sato's body just enough to slip the two grenades, their pins pulled, under the body. He sprinted back on board and got the rig back on the road. The phone was still connected. He picked it back up and gave TUSC an update.

"Package dumped." He called into the phone.

"Ok, one mile up the road there's an overpass with no median wall. Turn south on that. Once you do, lose the phone in the trees on the right. Here's the address. Be there in thirty minutes.

With that, the phone went dead. Matt made the U-turn at the overpass and ditched the phone.

As they headed south to the address TUSC had given him they passed the training center where only minutes earlier they had been discovering Sato's tattoos.

A parade of four black cars was leaving the cement instruction area and heading out the service road that they had just used.

Matt kept his focus on the road and the new time frame to get to the coordinates given to him by TUSC.

They were no more than a mile south of the airport when an audible explosion shook the air. Being this close to the airport one might think it was a possible sonic boom created by any number of military jet aircraft that frequently used JFK.

Matt knew better. There was a distinct difference between the sound of the sound barrier being broken and a couple of well-placed grenades going off.

Matt hoped that the explosion did enough damage to those tracking him to give him the time he needed to get where he was going. They no longer would have the tracking device that had been implanted in Sato's skin but they could still gain Intel in a traditional way to find a big RV leaving the airport service area through an unauthorized access point.

~

It is not well known that the Yakuza have members in the USA. It is well known to certain corporations that have fallen prey to their particular form of blackmail that they are alive and well and working in New York City.

Futoshi Okada had come to New York five years ago. He had been sent by his oyabun with orders to establish himself in New York and to use the skills of Yuki Sato, who they had recently persuaded to work exclusively for the Yakuza, to infiltrate Wall Street in any way they could. They did not care what methods

Futoshi used to gain access to accounts that Yuki could then hack and exploit.

Futoshi had made great headway with some smaller firms in the financial district and his business was gaining momentum. He had added a number of Kobun to his little group who were working out quite well in intimidating certain corporate playboys and gathering incriminating information on others who corporately had something to hide.

His biggest problem was with Yuki. The guy just couldn't stay put. He needed him to run the cyber-attacks on the servers of their unsuspecting prey but he was always looking for him. If there was a way Yuki could fuck up, he'd find it. There was too much for him to do here in America and he was not staying out of site. If he had his way, he would have made Yuki cut off part of his little finger but he had been told in no uncertain terms that Yuki needed his hands to perform his duties for the oyabun. Maybe he would cut his balls off. Maybe that would slow him down a bit.

Today was no different. He had a job for Yuki and he was just about to send a couple of his Kobun out to track him down when his phone buzzed and Yuki's number popped up.

"Where the fuck are you?" Futoshi asked. He was none too happy.

Futoshi listened for a minute barely containing his anger.

"You are a fucking idiot." He screamed into the phone. "I don't give a fuck that you have a backup plan. You should not have been there. Even if the sale was compromised you, at least, would not have been and you would not be running from an unknown."

Futoshi listened again for a few seconds before breaking in on Yuki's apology.

"It is only sheer luck that you have a way out. If you had been caught or killed it would not be your head it would also be mine. This I cannot allow. Get back here as fast as you can and hope I have calmed down enough to not cut off your ears when you do."

With that Futoshi disconnected the line and screamed at the top of his lungs.

He knew that it was already too late to send men to the dock house to try and recover the ivory. He only hoped Yuki would get his fucking ass back to New York so he could beat the living shit out of him.

He couldn't know that within a very short time he would be sending all of his hard-won troops out to find Yuki and the man who had taken him, prisoner.

TUSKS AND HANDGRENADES

The GPS lead them right to Sato's body. The men where assets loyal to Futoshi and were stationed in a warehouse a short distance from JFK. They mostly oversaw the comings and goings of certain containers bringing opium and other illegal substances into the states through a private air contractor.

Futoshi had set them on Sato's trail when he got the second call. This time with Sato screaming over top of the gunfire in the car, something about a helicopter chasing them.

Things had gone from bad to worse and as the phone went dead in mid-sentence, Futoshi decided it was to send in the troops.

They weren't hardened vets but they had been around. They knew when Futoshi gave them the word, it was, take no prisoners.

When they found Yuki lying on his stomach behind the crop of trees, two of the men left the cars to check if it was him and to see if he was dead.

One man, Taka, heard the two metal clicks as he pulled the dead weight over to see the crushed face and the broken body but he didn't equate them to what they were. Wasn't his fault really, he had grown up in the States and even though he had seen lots of combat and action movies where there were plenty of grenades flying around, he had never encountered one in real life.

Taka never knew what hit him. Neither did the other man who had foolishly accompanied him to check the body.

The rest got away mostly unscathed except for some lacerations from flying glass when the explosions took out all the side windows in the cars. If they had of parked a few feet closer that wouldn't have been their only problem.

They were not going to catch the fleeing motorhome. They didn't even know what it looked like. They only had Sato's GPS to track and the Intel from one of their subordinates who worked traffic control at JFK and had informed them of a very mysterious chopper drop off at the training center.

The tracking device had moved but only as far as the explosion had scattered Yuki.

It wasn't good and it wasn't going to get better when they reported to Futoshi that they had lost Sato and his captor.

It would be a huge blow to Futoshi's organization

and an even bigger blow to those in the Yakuza he worked for not to mention the millions that had been designated and promised to two very scary organizations in the middle east and one very mental Syrian president.

~

When the white five-ton van with Middlesex County Emergency Services pulled up to the end of the pier in Clinton, there was a small group of people milling about in front of what had been the overstock storage building for the marina. Recently, it had been bought by an offshore company which locals speculated was going to put in another restaurant to compete with the famous Shanks that had been the staple go-to seafood restaurant in Clinton for years.

The uneasy crowd became even edgier when they saw the HAZARDOUS MATERIALS RESPONSE scrawled along the side of the van and when the four-man team all dressed in yellow hazmat suits jumped out, the little group started to disperse.

One of the men from the van walked to those who still stood their ground.

"What's going on? Bill Matheson was the owner of the Harbor Side Marina and he was concerned that what he had thought was gunfire now looked to be something that might be even more detrimental to tourism in the area.

"Sir." The man in the yellow suit replied. "Have you seen or heard anything unusual in or around this building today?"

"Well, we all thought we heard gunfire. So some of us came down to have a look. I guess we thought better of going inside just in case." Bill replied.

"Smell anything in the air? Gas or chemical?"

"No, nothing unusual." Bill sounded worried.

"Ok," the man in the suit seemed calm. "It's probably nothing. The building is equipped with a GD1 Toxic Laser LOS Gas Detector. It sends a warning to our station if it detects even a miniscule amount of toxic gas in the air. It also tries to burn off any minor amounts before they can accumulate so as to give us a better response time. Probably the pops that you mistook for gunfire. Best you stand way back or go back to work. Well inform you if you need to leave the area but it doesn't look like it. If it was serious you would be dead by now."

Bill didn't waste any time in returning to the relative safety of the marina showroom. He adamantly hoped that he would not hear from the man in the yellow suit again.

When the cleanup crew frontman made his way into the building the rest of the crew had already made good progress.

He secured the front door just in case some of the residents decided they needed a closer look and dug in to help get the bodies ready for transport as fast as possible.

The beauty of the hasmat truck was they could back it right up to the doors and tarp the entire area off so their efforts would be totally hidden from prying eyes. Most onlookers gave them a wide birth when they thought there could be the potential for poisonous gas but you never knew.

The bodies were wrapped and quickly lifted into the back of the van. The two live targets followed along with the cleanup crew and approximately four million dollars in ivory. The bodies and the ivory would be off to the incinerator and the two live bodies to interrogation.

On the way past the marina, one of the hazmat team took a moment to poke his head in the door and let the owner know that it was a false alarm. He told him it looked like a fairly big muskrat had gotten stuck in one of the vents that circulated outside air and the detector had picked up the gasses from the bloated body. No worries and all good to go, he informed the marina owner.

It would be the talk of the town for almost two weeks.

BREAKFAST AT AMY'S

The Belt Parkway connected to the twenty-seven just south of the airport. Matt kept an eye on the traffic coming up behind but saw no immediate danger. The grenades must have done the job. He stayed on the twenty-seven until it turned into Ocean Parkway. Then followed that until it turned east and became the 278 which he followed until he turned off on Thirty-Ninth Street and pulled into the South Brooklyn Marine Terminal. His instructions were to follow the street to the gate at the end of the road. He would be given direction there.

The terminal was huddled in amongst six-story parkades, tenement housing, run down factories and sketchy apartment buildings. It would have looked almost abandoned if it weren't for the rows of new cars lined up on deck waiting to get transport to their respective dealers.

Matt pulled the RV to the gate and waited for the security guard to come to the door.

Matt saw him approach and hit the lever that slid the bus door open.

The guard just pointed to an open bay door in the side of a huge warehouse adjacent to the guard house, turned and walked away.

As he pulled the bus through the gate Matt noticed a couple of white hasmat trucks parked in a holding area on the other side of the guardhouse. His attention was only misdirected for a moment as he focused on getting the big RV through the door to the warehouse. It was just big enough to do so.

Once in, what appeared to be a rundown building from the outside was a bustling network of repair bays, all of which were in service. A flagman halfway down the row waved him toward one of the bays obviously designed for a vehicle the size of which Matt was driving.

Matt and the two of the medical team barely got out of the way before men in denim jeans and dirty white t-shirts had boarded the bus and were tearing out the medical equipment.

That was the first time Matt had ever seen TUSC in the works on American soil.

As the three stepped down from the RV they were met by a young man who looked exactly like the men taking the motorhome apart only slightly cleaner.

"Please come with me." He said,

They followed him to the bay door that they had
293

just brought the RV through and stood while the young man waved two waiting cabs over.

"These will take you home." He said and turned to walk back into the shop.

Matt was too tired to question the cab. He just got in the back, laid his head back and gave the driver his address in the city. He didn't even acknowledge the other two climbing into their waiting vehicle.

~

He must have fallen asleep. It seemed like only minutes and he was standing at his door in the city.

The cab ride had taken more than an hour in the traffic and it was starting to get dark. It had been a hell of a day and Matt barely made it to his bed before he was out cold.

Fully clothed, he slept until the next morning. He could feel the stress of the day before in his body. As he stood under a scalding hot shower, head the heat and the steam took him back to another shower high in the sky and the banter between him and Marianna in the field yesterday. He wondered where she was today if she was a permanent fixture of TUSC or an agent for hire as special needs required. He found he had a fond attraction to the smart, sexy woman who had been there when he needed support. His time with her yesterday, even though it was under duress, made him want to see her again.

It was almost eleven am before Matt had got himself dressed and felt awake enough to take a walk down to the little coffee shop at the corner of his street and Seventh Ave.

On his way out he decided to pop open his laptop and just check to see if there was any news about the crash he had caused the day before in his pursuit of Sato and the explosions he had left behind for those who were intent on Sato's recovery.

When the computer booted up an encrypted message jumped off the screen. Matt instantly decrypted it. One word. Call.

Matt quickly made his way down to the gift and souvenirs shop on Bleecker Street. The little shop had just about anything you could think of if you had to get a New York souvenir in hurry. T-shirts, postcards, shot glasses, you name it they had it. They also had cheap cell phones. Matt paid the lady behind the counter for the phone and a prepaid sim card and made his call.

When the call connected there was just silence on the other end so Matt said. "Yes."

"Information from the two packages and the photographs dropped off yesterday is if not incredible it's almost unbelievable," TUSC spoke in an almost hushed voice.

"How so?" Matt questioned.

"Two confirmations that it was Yuki Sato and imaging confirms that the graphics are what we thought. It might take some time to unravel but if we can we can shut down one of the most prolific money trains to three of the largest terror organizations in the world."

"When do we start?" Matt wanted to know.

"You don't until we have actionable Intel. Take the time to regroup and we'll be in touch. Just wanted you to know that this could be very significant. Good job."

With that, the line went dead.

As Matt walked along he broke the phone in two and pulled the sim card throwing one half in a trash can and the other down a grate in the street along with the sim card.

It was a beautiful day. The sun made its way lazily between the buildings on Bleecker Street and Matt took his time window shopping and letting the warm rays seep into his sweater and body.

He stopped for a moment to peek into the Bleecker Street Records store thinking how strange an actual album looked in its big cardboard envelope.

On the other side of the street, a small bakery and part-time coffee shop looked friendly and inviting. Matt could smell the freshly baked bread and his stomach started to grumble.

Amy's Bread was a cozy little place with a variety of fresh baked goods including bread and an array of local coffees. Matt bought a piece of freshly baked quiche and a large cup of steaming hot black coffee and settled into a seat at the window so he could watch the hustle and bustle of the street. One of his favorite things to do was watch the New York world go by. It had a calming effect for him to just watch people going about their day, oblivious to whatever else was going on in the world.

"Can I join you for a breakfast?" A soft female voice inquired.

Matt startled out of his reverie looked up into the smiling face of Marianna.

"How did you find me?

RENO

In Berthoud, a struggling father of three had been summoned by his sister to a meeting across the city. Normally this would have been out of the question for someone of Abdalla's stature. His meager earnings came from his part-time work as a cleaner at an auto transport facility. The big warehouse stored and maintained corporate vehicles, mostly larger transport trucks, between their various jobs.

The warehouse didn't have a cement floor but the dirt that the vehicles resided on had been packed down over the years so that it might as well have been.

Abdulla would systematically sweep the entire floor of the building three times a week. His pay barely kept his family in shelter and food but he was glad for the job and still started every day hopeful that a better opportunity would present itself.

This time, however, Abdulla's sister was insistent that he bring the family and stay for a celebration of their daughters sixteenth birthday.

He could not refuse and he had just finished his mid-week sweepathon at the warehouse so he would have two days to relax with family before he was needed back at work.

The trip across town took almost four hours on rickety buses that were more prone to breaking down than to making it to their intended destination in one piece but they finally arrived in time for the birthday celebration to begin. Abdulla was grateful that his children would be able to spend time with their cousins and he could use the time away to shake out some of the cobwebs and clear his own head. Besides, he had a great story to tell about the flaming white man that had blown through their door on a crazy looking scooter and had left wearing his one and only white shirt.

The two days went by quickly and Abdulla told his story of the man who had invaded their home. He did not repeat the story of the interrogation that followed his neighbor telling authorities about the unwanted intrusion. Their persistence as to who the man had been only diminished after Abdulla had convinced them that all he knew was that the man had come crashing through his door on a scooter followed by a huge boom and an extremely hot wind. When he and his family had recovered their hearing and thought it was safe to raise their heads the man had disappeared the way he had come in, minus his ride which was still leaning against the side of his home.

The authorities where still suspicious but could find no other reason to harass Abdulla so they had left him alone to try and track the suspect taking the half-baked scooter with them.

The trek home from his sisters was as tedious as the trip there. After a relatively relaxing two days of visiting Abdulla was not all that enthused about returning to his shitty job and his doorless home especially since he still hadn't been able to afford to replace it after it had been broken down during the explosion of the nearby warehouse.

The first thing he noticed as his family traipsed up their dreary little street was the brand new front door. He had been so engrossed with his musings about his job and lot in life that when he saw it he had to take a look around to see if he had made a mistake and walked down the wrong street.

A quick perusal of his surroundings confirmed that he had not taken a wrong turn but how could this have happened. His first emotion was one of fear. Had he done something to lose his house? Had it been repossessed and the new door would lock them out of their home. On turning the knob, he found that the door was open.

As he cracked it open, he looked around at his family and gave them a sign to stay back. He had no idea of how or why he would suddenly be the recipient of a new door. There could possibly be danger inside.

As the air from inside the house pushed its way past the brand new solid wood door Abdulla could smell the refined aroma of freshly cut wood with an underlying heaviness that he recognized as fresh paint on its way to drying.

He poked his head tentatively inside and as his eyes became accustomed to the gloom that was the general state of his home on any given day, he could not believe his what he saw. He turned once again to make sure he was not in someone else's building.

What had been slightly better than a hovel when he had left two days ago was now completely changed. His tiny world had been turned upside down.

The entire interior, main living area, what had passed as a bathroom and the two bedrooms, had been completely renovated. His once dirt floor was now wood and clay tile. A counter that actually held a sink and a tap had taken the place of a wooden stand with a precariously balanced bowl. The walls had been completely drywalled including the two bedrooms and the bathroom now had their own doors and unbelievably the bathroom had been converted with its own sink, shower, and wonder of all wonders a flush toilet.

Abdulla took one last look around the street just to make sure he hadn't stumbled into the wrong place before he opened the door to his family. Their screams of joy were dampened by the closing of the front door. It wouldn't do for Abdalla to have to explain to neighbors how he had accomplished this amazing transformation.

The door shut the family literally stood and stared. At the walls the floor and at each other. Abdalla's wife looked at him with a hundred questions on her face. Abdalla could only shrug. It was only after he had moved to the new sink, taking a moment to check the brand new refrigerator and stove that stood at the end of the beautiful counter, that he discovered the envelope with his name on it.

Just wanted to say thanks for your kindness when I invaded your privacy after the warehouse explosion. I hope this will pay for the shirt I cannot return.

Matt

Open mouthed Abdalla passed the envelop and note on to his wife and then as if in a daze moved through his new rooms, taking in all the things he thought he would never own. It was the sight of the four new white shirts sitting neatly on the beautiful new bed that brought tears to his eyes.

A FORD IN EVERY DRIVEWAY

The brand new Ford F150 had pulled into the driveway in the middle of the night. The engines turned off about half way up the block the driver had timed it perfectly to jump the small curb and silently come to rest right behind what appeared to be a piece of shit 2002 Toyota Avalon. It was exactly where the contractor said it would be. The driver had opened the door at the same time he had turned off the engine so when he stepped down out of the cab and shut the driver's door there wasn't even a click as it closed.

The F150 was the big black Limited Edition. There was just enough chrome to make it a bit menacing but not enough to take away the effect of the beautiful magnesium rims.

It was the 5.0 liter V-8 4X4 and it was loaded. It had everything you could get and then some. It also came with a manila envelope in the glove box filled with ten grand in cash.

The driver made sure the doors were locked and then tiptoed to the mailbox beside the front door of the poorly kept Cape Cod styled duplex. Truth be told, he had no idea why he was dropping off a

303

vehicle in the middle of the night that was likely worth as much as the whole friggin building but he was being paid really well for the job and there had been hints that if he pulled this off successfully there would be more work in the future.

He deposited the keys in the box with an accompanying letter and he was off down the street to a waiting car about six houses down. No one on the block noticed. It was a working-class neighborhood and morning came soon enough without getting up to investigate every passing car.

~

Martin's life and job had been pretty crazy since his insane run-in with the mysterious gunman and his, what he had been telling everyone, kidnapping at gunpoint and forced driving of the earth mover resulting in the accident and death of the men in the car.

He had become even more confused when the police finally tracked him down by the fact that the third victim of the car crash was not found until hours later in a picnic area near the airport. Even more confusing was the information that the third crash victim had been blown to bits with what authorities were claiming to be hand grenades.

It had taken many hours of interrogation and

convincing to persuade the police and his manager at work that he had been a helpless participant throughout the entire event and he had only complied at gunpoint.

The reports from motorists who had also been stopped by the bizarre scene on the highway, that day helped confirm that there had been another man in the earth mover with Martin and that the man had pulled one of the bodies from the wreckage, thrown it into a waiting helicopter and then fled the scene after jumping into an already airborne chopper.

That information had left the cops just shaking their heads and Martin could neither confirm nor deny that part of the event as he had taken off at a run as soon as he had found his legs and had not looked back. He had hoped that keeping his mouth shut, a virtue he had learned only too well back in the Czech Republic, would help him stay invisible until officers showed up at the office of the construction company he worked for with a pretty good artist's rendering of one of the suspects in the incident.

At first, the company had flat out fired him. They couldn't have the controversy that came with the incident. He would have to go and good luck to him finding work in the same vocation elsewhere.

Since then, fortunes had turned somehow. The

manager had phoned and apologized for his hasty firing and asked him to take a few days off before returning to work and even though Martin could not think of why the boss had changed his mind he was grateful nonetheless.

This morning as he stepped out his front door, he was just on his last day off before returning to work and had decided to hit one of the local beaches and just sit and watch the waves come in. With any luck, there would be a cute bikinied girl here and there to take his mind off of the past two weeks.

The first thing he noticed as he stepped down from the door sill was a white envelope protruding from the top of his mailbox. He opened the lid and peered in. The envelope was attached to a key fob along with a couple of shiny new keys. Martin tentatively slid the envelope out of the box along with the keys and with head down began walking toward the driveway.

He had the letter half open when he stopped short in his tracks. There in the driveway was the truck of his dreams. The one he had thought of every day since leaving his homeland for the United States. It must be some kind of a joke. Maybe a neighbor?

As he stood wondering what the hell, he extracted the note from the envelope and began to read.

"Hey Martin, got your creds from the job application you filled out with your company. Thought you might be persona non grata after our little adventure the other day, so I sent you a little something to make up for the experience. Don't worry it's all legal and paid for. The license and ownership are in the glove box.

Thanks for your help."

Martin just sat down on the lawn. All he could think was, "Only in America."

THE KOMODO DRAGON

T.U.S.C.

The tattoo of the Komodo dragon was intimately and intricately wrapped around itself. Every detail of the outer skin had been woven into a writhing, seething whirlwind of tooth and scale, curled tongue and taloned claw all of which becoming part of the other as the layers folded in on themselves to create what could only be described as a work of art.

What made the dragon even more astounding was that it was on the back of a dead man. Not just his back but almost his entire back including his arms, legs, and neck. It was a compliment to the skill of the tattooist that when one first approached the life-sized image on the naked body, it seemed almost real. Not even the use of bright reds, yellows, and greens that were not common to the real-life Komodo dragon took away from the illusion.

The most extraordinary element of the tattoo was that buried within the lines and so craftily aligned with the patterns of scale, tooth, and claw, that they escaped only the most focused scrutiny, was code. Lines and lines of code.

The forensic team at TUSC had to use a light microscope to make sure they got all the leading edges of each number as some were so closely made that they looked conjoined. Whoever had done the tattooing would have had to of done so with the same type of magnifying glass to get the code so small. They would have also had to have used some kind of customized needle to manage such tiny imagery without blurring the edges.

They knew what they were looking at. It was an accounting of every digital transaction, money exchange and bank account for which Yuki Sato had control of for the Yakuza gang he must have been a member of. Somehow the gang had found a way to make Yuki their bitch.

There was only one reason why Yuki had spent so much time and a shit load of money to get this much data and tattooing on his back, safety net. He had put all the numbers on his back so the gang would have his back, so to speak.

While the whole world was hiding their files with encrypted locks, secure hard drives and hack-proof data storage, Yuki had gone old school. Everything anyone needed to know to totally collapse this particular Yakuza gang and those that would be found out by following the money, was hidden in plain sight carved into a Komodo Dragon tattoo on the back of the now lifeless body of Yuki Soto. So much for a backup plan.

When the code was decoded, it would send TUSC's singular agent on his most daring undercover operation ever.

~

After working together to run down and implode an ivory smuggling ring with links to Middle East terror organizations and the Yakuza, Matt had spent a week with Marianna, an agent for hire sometimes used by TUSC, who had helped save his bacon a couple of times in the past month.

They had wandered the streets of New York, caught a couple of off-Broadway plays and generally just unwound after the last mission.

Matt had made several attempts in the last few days to coerce Marianna's last name out of her but to no avail. She told him that after being so careless as to give his home address to a cab driver within earshot of someone who could potentially lead the wrong person to his doorstep, how could she possibly give him information that might compromise her?

A point well-taken and one that Matt upon hearing how she had tracked him down, would not forget.

After Marianna had left, Matt called his old mentor Ethan, just for a chat and a catch-up. He always came away from their conversations feeling a little more settled and grounded. While he couldn't give Ethan any details of what he had been doing, he could relate his stress levels and Ethan would remind him of some Zen exercises to calm himself and get back to center.

The rest of the week, he spent his mornings at a dojo in his neighborhood working on his katas and generally pulling himself together after so many days away.

Matt had to be careful. If anyone at the dojo got a sense of his ability it would not be a good thing. The art was widespread across America but the community was still small. Someone with his skill set would stick out like a sore thumb and would soon draw unwanted attention.

Still, the dojo was mostly quiet at certain times of the day and he stayed to himself. He was still officially on leave but he knew once they had decoded the tattoos on the back of the Yakuza hacker he had killed, he would be tasked with finding one if not all of the uncovered offenders. He also knew that the New York chapter of whatever Yakuza gang Yuki Sato had been a member of would be looking for him. They would not give up that quest so easily and if they caught wind of some white guy with ninja skills working out in an out of the way dojo in New York, that might be something they would want to investigate.

James Kelly